Also by Brittani Louise Taylor

A Sucky Love Story:
Overcoming Unhappily Ever After

Saintsville

Brittani Louise Taylor

PERMUTED
PRESS

A PERMUTED PRESS BOOK
ISBN: 978-1-68261-910-0
ISBN (eBook): 978-1-68261-911-7

Saintsville
© 2020 by Rex Films LLC
All Rights Reserved

Cover design by William Hyler
Interior layout and design by Sarah Heneghan,
sarah-heneghan.com

Permuted Press, LLC
New York • Nashville
permutedpress.com

Published in the United States of America

To the Eves of the world, you are more special than you know. And to the Maggies, don't change a thing.

Chapter 1

I can't go to sleep.

If I go to sleep, they will come.

Four white walls. A bed. A door. That is what I see. Day after day after day. Except when they come for me, then I see something else.

Teeth chattering, I am afraid.

Standing in the middle of my room—my cage—my legs have gone numb. They tingle and shake. Tilting my head to look above, the fluorescent lights flicker.

The laugh that escapes is bitter.

I am like that light now. On and off. Dark and light. Precariously close to dimming forever.

It's always so cold in here. My filthy hospital gown thin and mocking.

I am alone. Left alone, but never for long.

They wait.

They watch.

When I am quiet. When I am weak. When my eyes are closed and I am dreaming dreamless dreams, that is when they make their move.

Hypnotized by the fluttering light dancing between my lashes, everything starts to dim. With a crash, I fall to the floor.

My head hits last, echoing on the solid concrete surface.

Only then does the door open, and they come.

All I can do is scream.

"No!" Eve shrieks, eyes snapping open. Her skull feels like it's splitting in two. The sun's rays bouncing off the hood blind her as she throws up her hands, hiding from the light. Grabbing onto the first thing she touches, she hangs on for dear life. Another set of fingers latches onto hers, digging their nails into her skin as she yanks. She realizes she is in a car as it veers left, then right, coming dangerously close to a poorly constructed barrier hugging the two-lane deserted freeway.

"Eve? What the hell, you psycho! Let go!" shrieks a woman's voice beside her. Eve knows that voice, as a solid slap connects, distracting her long enough for the driver to successfully dislodge her grip.

Eyes focusing, she recognizes the shaking driver. White knuckles firmly clench the steering wheel as the redhead scowls at her, guiding them back into the center of the lane.

It's her sister. Maggie.

And with that, she crumbles. Dawning realization hits as Eve sits frozen in the passenger seat.

Dream. It was all just a dream. And afterwards, she woke up, grabbed the steering wheel, and almost killed them both.

Groaning, she slides down on the cracked leather, burying her pounding head in her hands. She doesn't know whether to laugh, cry, or apologize profusely while doing both. Embarrassment heats Eve's pale face, the blood warming her pale cheeks.

Boom, boom, boom, her heart pounds. Minutes pass before she feels it start to slow. Her ragged breathing calming to an even inhale and exhale.

Everything felt so real! She was in that room—she was emaciated, afraid, and alone. And she was terrified of what was waiting outside that door. But what did she see? What had been coming for her? The details of her vivid nightmare are already starting to escape, leaving Eve like a house with no furniture. Uncomfortable and empty.

Taking a deep breath, she exhales.

Her head collides with the glass pane as Maggie floors it, swinging back into the opposite lane and then careening to the right.

"Ouch! What the heck?" Eve exclaims, but Maggie ignores her. The car violently jerks up and down as it leaves the safety of the asphalt, connecting with rugged potholes. Slamming on the brakes, they come to a complete stop. A cloud of dust chases them down, surrounding the classic automobile.

Her little sister jumps out of the car, throwing the door shut behind her. *Slam.*

Eve's heart pounds once more. Not because of fear this time, but outrage. Maggie didn't even give her a chance to explain before pulling this stunt.

Eve pauses, wondering how to calmly explain to someone that you think you might be losing your mind. Red curls bounce as Maggie stomps around the front bumper, only halting when she's planted firmly outside the passenger side. Raising one of her combat boots, she kicks the front tire. More than likely fantasizing about her foot connecting with something other than rubber.

Shaking her head, Eve realizes that hours before—when she was thinking about how things couldn't possibly get any worse on this road trip—she was wrong.

They had already been fighting across two…no, correction, *three* state lines. Yes, seizing the wheel of a moving vehicle during the aftermath of a nightmare was not her most shining moment. As much as Eve wants to justify her actions, she is drawing a blank as to "why." All that she knows is that she woke up, panicked, and ironically enough, is about to be berated for her stupidity by her younger sibling.

Not that Eve is surprised. Life has a way of continually letting her down.

Maggie's small palm smacks against the window, causing Eve to jump. The harsh afternoon light casting her curves into silhouette.

"Get out!" Maggie rasps, slamming her fist this time against the glass barrier.

How did their lives come to this?

Straightening, Eve grinds her teeth as she manually unlocks the door, pulling the handle. The hinges creak as she exits, squinting at their rusted excuse for transportation.

All you needed to do was look at the pile of mismatched boxes filling the back end of their car, and take in their threadworn clothing, to know that both of these women had landed on hard times. As much as Eve isn't in the mood for more confrontation, she knows she has to make things right with, quite literally, the only person she has left.

"You!" Maggie paces back and forth, hurling her words like stones. "What the heck were you thinking? You don't…do that!"

Maggie pulls her right arm back and then hurls the object in her hand. Her sister barely has time to register a set of keys as they whiz dangerously close to her temple, causing her to squeal and duck. Her glasses fly to the ground, their absence immediately impairing Eve's already-poor vision. Blindly patting the dirt, she locates her spectacles near her feet, wiping the dust off the lenses with the bottom of her shirt.

Firmly planting them back onto the bridge of her nose, Eve rises once more, flustered.

"We have one set of keys! One! And where is our...one... set...of keys? Now, thanks to you, somewhere out there!" Eve stabs the air with her finger, pointing over her shoulder.

Not waiting for Maggie's response, she turns, scanning the dried foliage and cacti for a flash of silver—any clue, really, that would indicate where they might have landed.

Maggie's hand roughly turns her older sister back to face her.

The two of them are total opposites.

Eve is tall and gangly, while Maggie is a foot shorter and nothing but curves. Eve has dark brown locks, shoulder-length and stick-straight, with messy bangs framing her square lenses. Maggie, a natural ginger, boasts a lion's mane full of red curls— thick and unruly, cascading down her back. With her heart-shaped face, the youngest Abbott could have been straight out of a Renaissance painting...minus the nose ring and heavy coal lining her eyes.

Their eyes are their only resemblance. Bright blue and clear, cementing the fact that they are, indeed, related.

"What the hell was what? Do you seriously have a death wish?" Maggie demands, her voice cracking.

"I'm sorry...." Eve mumbles, staring at her dirty Converse.

Now pacing, Maggie croaks, "Just 'sorry'?"

"Yes, sorry. This is me, expressing remorse for my actions."

By this point, Maggie is so worked up she can hardly speak. Unshed tears glisten as she backs away, putting distance between them in more ways than one.

"Unbelievable...you...find...keys...I'm gonna sit...in...stupid...car."

Her entrance back into the vehicle is just as dramatic as her exit, the driver's side door slamming closed once more.

Looking to the barren desert in which they are now stranded, and back to her little sister's rigid form inside the car, Eve decides to take her chances with the landscape.

Surprising herself, she snorts.

The giggles turn into full on belly laughs, and once Eve starts, she can't stop. The absurdity of the situation is just too much.

"If you are going to lose our keys on purpose, could you not pick a hot wasteland in the middle of nowhere?" Eve yells, making sure Maggie hears every syllable. Rolling her eyes, Maggie flips Eve the bird, which only sets Eve off further. Wiping the moisture from her eyes, the eldest Abbott eventually sobers. The keys aren't going to find themselves, and the setting sun would only further complicate her search.

First, false hope as she chases a reflection, mistaking a gum wrapper for them. Then, while perusing near a particularly large boulder, a snake decides to join in on her quest. Is it poisonous? Is she really in any sort of danger? She doesn't bother checking before letting out a yelp and scrambling to the very top of a large boulder.

Which now, with a reptile somewhere below it, feels all too small. If the universe is trying to further punish Eve for her actions, it's succeeding.

Witnessing the whole ordeal—minus the possibly dangerous reptilian part—Maggie rolls down her window and bellows, "What the heck are you doing?"

"There's a snake!" Eve squeals, pulling her knees to her chest. She frantically examines the ground, scanning for any kind of movement.

"Did it bite you?"

"No!"

"Darn. Not my lucky day...."

"Maggie!"

"Kidding. Still nothing?"

"What do you think...."

"I think I feel sorry for the snake. At least he's next to you, and not me!"

"Here's a thought. Come and help?"

Maggie's turn to laugh.

"Ha, no way...."

Manually forcing the window back up, Maggie shifts, unsticking her body from the seat. Windows down would probably grant her an occasional breeze, but she needs total silence to be able to think. Sure, she really should go help look. It'll be getting dark soon, and the last thing Maggie wants is to spend the night in this car. But, if she's being honest with herself, she's kind of afraid of the gangly nerd currently stranded on a large rock. Sometimes there are worse things in life than snakes or lost keys. Eve is cracking. Her solid, always-reliable, by-the-book, boring-but-loveable older sister is falling apart at the seams.

And Maggie blames herself.

She knows that she hasn't made things easy on her sister the past few years. Her rebellious nature usually equates to breaking the rules, but maybe she's pushed Eve too far? Maggie feels like a Titanic-size weight was put on her sister when she was left in Eve's care. Eve's love for her is a given, but Maggie knows what a huge roadblock she's become to her sister's future.

Could she really blame Eve for looking for an exit?

It's a morbid thought, but neither of them really has much left to lose.

Digging into a trash bag at her feet bursting with unwashed laundry, Maggie buries her face in the musty fabric of a dirty flannel, wishing she could wipe away this day as easily as the perspiration on her forehead.

By the time Eve finds the keys on the other side of the boulder and makes it back to the car, forty-five minutes have passed, and two things have happened.

One, since Maggie insisted on sitting in the hot station wagon while her sister scoured alone, she is covered in sweat. And two, she is definitely in a better mood. The moisture coating her skin must have put out a bit of her emotional fire.

To Eve's surprise, Maggie declines the keys, putting Eve behind the wheel. A test, maybe, to see if Eve has managed to pull herself together? The engine struggles as it carries them onto the solid pavement once more, as Eve feels a light tap on her freshly sunburnt forearm.

A water bottle.

She gladly accepts, drinking greedily. They haven't seen another car in hours. Apparently, they are among the brave few to venture this far south into the Arizona landscape.

A comfortable silence descends as they drive…or as comfortable as it can be when nothing has really been resolved. Eve may be twenty-two, and Maggie sixteen, but they're still siblings. Like most siblings, power struggles often ensue. Eve, older and more patient, only needs to wait.

As predicted, Maggie surrenders first. Kicking off her boots, she rests her bare feet on the glovebox. Grabbing her bra straps behind her tank top, she gives them a snap before turning her head toward her sister.

"Well, what gives?" Maggie demands.

Eve shifts uncomfortably. "Honestly, I...I don't know," she stutters, at a loss on how to explain her temporary insanity.

Remembering something, Maggie's mouth turns up into a knowing smile.

"Well, you were moaning like a cow in labor."

"I was not!"

"Oh yeah, you were! If you're gonna have a 'sexy' dream, do you mind waiting until I'm not within earshot? I think I'm permanently scarred...."

"I wasn't..." Eve begins in a whisper, her reddened cheeks flushing further.

"Uh-huh, sure. Whatever you were doing or not doing, no judgment. Been there, and *definitely* done that. Just try not to wake up and violently attack me? Especially not while I'm driving a moving vehicle...." Maggie stops there. Digging her cracked iPod out of her backpack, she unrolls her headphones and pops them in her ears, effectively ending the conversation before it has even started.

No surprise there.

Eve could count the number of "heart to heart" conversations they've had over the years on one hand. Still, she thought Maggie had let her off the hook pretty easily—minus the car-keys treasure hunt. And if she is being honest, Eve really doesn't want to discuss the matter further. She's already buried so much in her life, what is one more memory?

Goosebumps cover Eve's arms, despite the desert heat.

Eve knows.

In that moment, she *knows* that this will happen again. This nightmare is the first, but it most certainly won't be the last. How is she going to distinguish what's real? Asleep, it felt like she was awake, and awake, she wonders if this could possibly be a dream?

Her brooding is interrupted by a city sign manifesting in the distance, gradually growing in size as they approach. The small billboard is weathered and peeling as Eve struggles to make out the words through her thick lenses. Coming into focus, faint black letters on a simple blue background form to say:

Saintsville

Population: 140

"Correction, one hundred and forty-two. Aren't we lucky?" Maggie mumbles over the heavy metal blasting her eardrums.

The old placard is right in front of them and then gone, left behind before they've had a chance to really study it. Not that there was much to see. Wood, paint, lettering. A reassuring landmark, letting them know that their journey is coming to an end.

"One hundred and forty-two? That can't be right. They probably haven't bothered updating it…" Eve soothes, trying to infuse some hope into their situation. Most days, Eve is like a balloon—and Maggie, a needle. It's not surprising what happens when they collide.

"Welcome to hell," Maggie states, popping Eve's fragile optimism.

"Welcome home…" Eve whispers.

And she prays that, for once, she's right.

Chapter 2

As they drive, the landscape starts to slowly morph. Juniper trees, if Eve had to guess, stretch as far as she can see, except for large gaps in the forest where farms have taken residence. The closer they get to Saintsville, the stronger Eve's feeling of déjà vu. Which is strange, because the Abbott sisters have never been anywhere. Literally. Their parents were both professors with demanding positions at a prestigious university. Maggie and Eve spent more time with babysitters growing up than they did with their biological caregivers.

Still, just thinking about Adel and Orion, their mother and father, cuts deep.

Eve and Maggie are technically orphans.

They usually avoid explaining this part of their history if they can. Eve was eighteen, having just graduated high school. At the time, Maggie was only twelve. Her younger sister has always been loud and opinionated, but she was different back then…softer. Her smiles were effortless and her laughter abundant. Now, the best word to describe Maggie would be…jaded.

Switching on the headlights as dusk makes its appearance, Eve falls back into thoughts of their turbulent past.

It was October. Houses in their neighborhood were covered in festive Halloween decorations, even more extravagant than when it was Christmastime. Eighteen-year-old Eve was carving pumpkins at her best friend Lily's house, a tradition they did every year. She recalls a loud knock at the door, and Lily's dad answering. Voices rumbled, the words indistinct. Her name was called, and with that, Eve quickly abandoned her jack-o'-lantern, curious to see why she was being summoned.

The look on Lily's dad's face said it all.

Escorted to a squad car, the cop promised to explain once they arrived at the station. Maggie looked so tiny and fragile, already waiting in the back seat.

Eve remembers holding her hand as silent tears slid down her sister's beautiful face.

Everything after that was a blur. A female detective, Eve couldn't remember her name, but she was blonde, in her forties, with weathered features. She was kind as she broke the news. Something had happened to their parents. They had found debris and their blood scattered in their laboratory, indicating that there had been a brutal attack.

What they hadn't found, thankfully, were their parents' bodies. The authorities believed that they might still be alive. They waited for a ransom to be demanded. They waited for new evidence to be discovered.

Four years later, the police have long since given up their search, but Eve and Maggie are still waiting, tortured by their lack of answers.

Their parents are gone, and as time passes, more than likely it's for good.

Thankfully, Adel and Orion had savings set aside, but that only lasted a year or two. Eve is now not only Maggie's sister, but assigned by the court to be her legal guardian—something she would lose if her ineptitude is ever discovered. Homeless and broke didn't exactly scream "responsible adult." Hence, leaving the only home they have ever known and moving here. To Saintsville. Hopefully here, they will be able to start over.

They sold their parents' cars first. Correction—their nice cars. The station wagon isn't anything to brag about, but it's reliable. No matter what happens, it always turns on. It always keeps running.

Orion took them camping in it once. That was a good trip. A good memory, which in turn created a certain fondness toward this particular vehicle, despite its appearance.

Next, they sold all the furniture but their beds. When that wasn't enough to keep them afloat, they kept selling, until the only items that remained were in the tattered boxes now traveling in back. For Eve, her treasures are her books. Printed words are the enemy of her poor eyesight, but they are the only place she can escape. In those books, she can be anyone, do anything, and for a little while, forget.

Eve is smart. Smart enough to have earned a full ride to college, but an incomplete degree in English didn't pay the bills. She chose Maggie over finishing, putting food on the table over a degree. Not that it made much difference, she thinks, looking at the moody young adult beside her. After their parents' disappearance, Maggie pretty much ran wild. And frankly, at the time, Eve was in too much pain to care. She wasn't ready to be a parental figure. When it came to raising Maggie, Eve had screwed up. Only one of the many ways, when it came to Maggie, she has fallen short.

Even working three jobs wasn't enough to keep them from drowning.

Saving her tears for when she's finally alone, Eve tries to distract herself, studying the landscape. The change from desert to forest is a welcome one. Already it feels more like Seattle, and Eve can see why their grandmother loved it here.

June used to visit once a year and spoiled them both with love and presents. Adel's mother was the opposite of her daughter. Free spirited, where Adel had been uptight and strict. Affectionate and loud, her optimism was contagious. Eve and Maggie loved her, but only as much as you can love someone who isn't a constant in your life.

June was murdered a month before their parents' disappearance. Exactly how she was killed had never been disclosed. That was just how their parents had operated. Everything was on a need-to-know basis, and Adel and Orion felt that their daughters would only be hurt further by the truth. Not that it stopped Eve from digging. She scoured the *Sainstville Gazette* obituaries and repeatedly called their police station. Never receiving a straight answer, sadly, her sleuthing was to no avail.

More pain fills Eve's chest at the thought of Grandma June. Adel and Orion had been too busy in their research to even consider attending her funeral.

What could have possibly been more important?

Sometimes Eve wonders if there is a curse on their family.

Another weathered, faded, blue sign comes into view, drawing Eve back to reality.

"Left, Saintsville High, and right, downtown," Maggie reads aloud. "You're right, Eve, this town has *totally* grown over the years! Rumor has it, they're gonna add a third arrow, pointing back the direction we came, and it'll say, 'leave while you still can!'"

Maggie tosses her curls and huffs. Apparently, something about the scenery sets her on edge as well.

"Do you want to go by Jill's first? Or maybe explore a bit?" Eve asks, changing the subject.

"I'm serious. Let's find a gas station, fill the wagon up, and then go home. Yay! Road trip, sister bonding time was a total blast, but I'm done," Maggie states sarcastically. She has been begging Eve to go back to Washington ever since they left. Her friends are there, her now-ex-boyfriend is there, Eve is ruining her life, and so on, and so on....

"What part of 'we are broke' don't you get? There is no returning to Seattle. At least not yet. Jill has offered us a free place to live and me steady work. Whether you realize it or not, I am trying to do what is best for you!" Eve placates.

"Mom and dad hated Aunt Jill...no clue why, but still! We haven't seen her in, what, over ten years? Maybe we should just trust their judgment—"

"Stop. Maggie," Eve interrupts. "Please, stop! Enough. We are homeless. Without this, we have no money and no place to stay. It's this, or nothing."

"But—"

"I think we're here!" Eve states with finality.

Relief fills her as a small town starts to reveal itself among the trees.

Charming. Quaint? Saintsville feels like it has been lost in time. The residents have chosen to restore the vintage buildings, keeping their original charm intact. Bricks and fabric awnings. Old glass with even older-style lettering proclaims the names of the businesses. Post Office. Saintsville Market. Angel's Boutique, a clothing store. Eve counts no more than twenty establishments as she searches for their first stop.

"There it is, up on the right!" she points, spotting Jill's Coffee Shop. Pulling into a parking spot out front, their headlights shine on the Closed sign hanging on the red-trimmed door. Checking the time on the dash, it is only a little past seven, but they're one of only two cars parked on the vacant street.

"Are you sure she's here?" Maggie questions. Eve can tell that she is nervous, watching her pick at the deep red nail polish on her thumb.

"She said to come to the back and knock." Not waiting for her sister, Eve gets out and stretches. It's been a long trip, made longer by the whole bad-dream, lost-keys fiasco. And Eve, like her sister, is uneasy. Walking up to the front of the café, she takes it in. White and red is Jill's chosen color scheme, beyond the brick exterior. Cupping her hands to the glass, she peeks into the dimly lit bistro. She notices individual tables with red tablecloths and old white metal chairs and a small, currently empty display case for baked goods connected to a white counter. There's even a huge chalkboard hanging above it with a handwritten menu—upon it, a list of sandwiches and various popular coffee drinks.

Thanks to the streetlights, Eve can see her reflection faintly in the windows. Straightening her spectacles, she strategically uses her bangs to cover a bruise on her forehead—a gift from Maggie when she swerved, causing Eve's head to connect with the glass.

Eve studies her face for a moment before retrieving a scrunchie from her wrist and gathering the rest of her hair up into a ponytail. Checking her reflection once more, she frowns. Dark circles are stark against her white skin. Her arms and legs are swimming in her clothing. She's too thin, stress probably playing its part. Eve looks like she feels—unable to hide the toll fate has dealt her.

Maggie swiftly approaches, grabbing her hand and tugging until her sister's feet start to move once more. As they round the corner, a light on the wall a little ways down illuminates another red door, solid in shape. This must be what Jill had meant.

Maggie charges ahead toward the door, but Eve freezes. A whisper of air tickles the back of her exposed neck, sending cold chills down her spin. Turning to look, there is nothing behind her. Nothing but the quiet buildings in this quiet town.

Her stomach tightens. She can't shake the feeling that they are being watched.

Chapter 3

"Eve...Eve? Hello, Earth to Eve!" Maggie shouts, her voice somewhere in the background. Eve is still turned toward the road, the hairs on her arms raised.

Eve has always believed that we're born with certain basic senses. Smell, touch, taste. But there are others. Warning bells wired into our very DNA. As we get older, we tend to ignore our natural-born instincts. Blowing them off, making excuses for our fear or unease. In that moment, Eve's only thoughts are of protecting Maggie. She isn't frozen in fear, she's waiting.

Feeling a tap on her shoulder, she whips around, startled by Maggie's presence for the second time that day.

"Look, you weirdo. I'm hungry. I'm tired. Let's knock, get the keys, and go," Maggie grumbles, annoyed, but her eyes are laced with concern. Not wanting to have to explain, the eldest Abbott wordlessly pushes Maggie to the door. Keeping herself between Maggie and the threat she can't explain, she glances once more over her shoulder.

Whatever she'd felt is suddenly gone. Imaginary or real, the threat has passed.

When they reach the crimson doorway, Eve realizes it's been freshly painted. Jill is obviously a stickler for perfection, from the inside out. Not waiting for her sister, Maggie finds a small doorbell to the right of the frame and pushes. A loud, solid buzzer resonates from inside the brick walls. Within moments they hear footsteps approaching. From the sound of it, thick-soled boots.

Eve's stomach churns, this time with nervous anxiety. The door flies open, and a pretty redhead peeks her head from around the corner.

Jill.

Taking in the girls, she squeals in delight and throws her arms around Maggie. Not much has changed since they last saw her. Now in her mid-thirties, Jill matches Eve in height, but where Eve is tall and lean, Jill is solidly muscled. Maggie awkwardly pats Jill on the back, trapped in her embrace. The family resemblance between the two is undeniable. Maggie and Jill acquired the same recessive genes, gifting them with matching red curls. If anything, Jill looks like she could be Maggie's mother, minus her chocolate-brown eyes. Noticing Eve, she releases Maggie and greets her with the same gusto. A giant hug and quiet sob, betraying the weight their family estrangement must have placed.

Relaxing, Eve wraps her arms around her aunt, realizing just how much she has missed her.

Wiping tears from her eyes, Jill finally lets go of Eve and grabs both of her nieces' hands, pulling them through the doorway into what looks like a kitchen. More equipped as a bakery, there are various different types of ovens, with a large prep table firmly planted in the middle. Squinting in the semi-darkness, Eve takes in the white, shelf-lined walls, holding plastic containers with necessary ingredients. Flour, sugar, dried fruits, candies, and nuts. Releasing their hands, Jill motions toward a room past the kitchen on the right, which Eve guesses to be an office. The lights are on, and as soon as she steps inside, she sees her assumption is spot-on.

It's a simple, windowless room, which Jill has obviously tried to make as homey as possible. There's an antique wooden desk in back with manila folders stacked and organized. On the wall to the right, a clock with a mounted rack holding three heavily stamped timecards—probably for her employees. Another shelf boasts pictures of Jill in a baseball cap, her arm thrown casually around a man who's holding up a sizeable fish. Yet another image catches Eve's eye and she pauses. Without thinking, she moves toward it and gently picks up the frame with one hand, while the other pushes her horn-rimmed glasses back up the bridge of her nose.

The photo is of them. Maggie and Eve when they were younger. They had to be...five and eleven? She recalls this particular memory well. Maggie had gotten into trouble—for god knows what. It was Maggie, after all. She had convinced Eve to help her rake up the leaves in the front yard, her parental-designated punishment. But Maggie—again, being Maggie—kept jumping into the leaf pile, scattering Eve's hard work across the grass. Fed up, Eve grabbed Maggie, pinning her arms to her sides, and they both had tumbled into the woodsy pile.

Laughter. Both wheezing so hard they couldn't breathe, and their dad had witnessed the entire debacle from the kitchen window. He ran out holding a vintage polaroid camera. *Flash.*

That...was a good day.

"How did you get this?" Eve asks, curious. Jill plops down at her desk, her black Doc Martens resting on the wood surface as she leans backwards in her chair.

"Your mom sent it to me for my birthday one year. She knew how much I missed both of you...." Clearing her throat, Jill looks away. A flash of pain is written on her features before she recovers, falling back into a warm, mischievous grin.

Maggie, already over their reunion, wastes no time. "It's great to see you, really. I'm ecstatic. Cool photo. But can we get what we need, and like, get out of here?" Her words are laced with sarcasm, but thankfully, Jill doesn't seem to notice. Springing into action, their aunt plops her feet back down and opens a drawer next to her desk, taking out a set of old keys on a rusty, silver lightning-bolt keychain.

Walking straight past the sisters, Jill returns to the kitchen and they follow. Their aunt pulls open the door of a large refrigerator, face briefly illuminated as she takes out two paper bags, their names individually scribbled on each. Sheepishly, she hands them over, giving Eve the keys as well. Wiping her fingers on her ripped jeans, she retreats.

"I figured my nieces might be hungry after such a long trip. Maggie, ham and cheese for you, no mayo. And Eve, turkey on rye? I think that's what you girls used to like...." she mutters, walking toward the door in which they came.

What happened that was so bad that their mother cut this sweet woman completely out of their lives? As generous as Jill seems, and as much as Eve desperately wants to reconnect with their only living blood relative, she can't help but feel wary. Their parents had to have a good reason, and she needs to continue to trust their judgment.

Hugging the girls once more, Jill pulls a crinkled piece of paper from her pocket. It's a hand-drawn map, with clear directions to their grandmother's home.

She really had thought of everything.

"Turn right, stay on Saints Street for fifteen or so until you come to a big lake. It's a quick left from there onto Red Creek Road, and Mom's will be on the left. Big and white, you can't miss it! I'll call you on the landline in the morning." The red door closes as she speaks, until it clicks shut.

"Night Jill, thank you…" Eve says politely, hoping their aunt could hear her still from the other side. Heading back toward the car, she's forgotten all about her earlier trepidation. Flashes of their childhood and past begin to drown out any other previous musings. Both girls are silent, lost in their shared history. Their sandwich bags softly crinkle in their hands as they walk, Maggie stopping outside the driver's-side door.

"Keys," she demands, holding out her free hand as Eve rounds the other side and tosses. Maggie catches them with ease, opens the car, and crawls across the seat to unlock Eve's side. There are no power locks in their old, trusty station wagon.

Eve studies the directions for a moment as Maggie turns on the headlights and throws their car in reverse. Stomachs rumbling, they empty the contents of their bags and devour the food ravenously. Her little sister drives with her knees, expertly navigating and chewing. The bread is homemade and fresh. Only Jill could turn a sandwich into a work of art. Eve had forgotten what a good cook Jill was.

Correction—is.

And the icing on the cake is her famous kitchen-sink cookies (called so because, you guessed it, they contain everything but the kitchen sink). Mouth-wateringly delicious, the desserts are a welcome surprise in the bottom of the bag.

As they eat and drive, the heavy forest lining either side of the now-dirt road feels massive and imposing. Like the sisters are intruding. Their automobile is tiny when compared to the magnitude of the tall stumps and long branches. They have never stayed anywhere this remote or been in a city devoid of streetlights. From the looks of it, where they were headed, they were going to be living in isolation.

"I think that's the lake up there?" questions Eve, leaning forward and squinting. Her eyesight had been getting worse, but she hadn't been able to afford to go to the optometrist.

Following Jill's directions, they make a sharp left.

"That's a lake, alright. But why do they call it 'Red Creek' Road? There's no creek, from what I can see.... Wait, people in this town know the difference between a creek and a lake, right?"

"I can ask Jill?" Eve suggests, making a mental note.

"Ugh. Jill. I can't stand her...."

Laughing, Eve responds, "You can't stand anyone!"

"This is true," her sister admits, without a shred of shame.

"We barely know her, Maggie. Don't you think we should give her a chance before making up our minds?" That's what Eve had decided—to reserve judgment until knowing all the facts. In their limited time spent with Jill during visits, she had always been loving and thoughtful.

"Look, Mom cut her off for a reason. Our dearly deceased—we think—mother wanted nothing to do with her. So I think I'll pass."

Stubborn to the core, Eve thinks, but Maggie does have a point. The trees start to thin out, revealing a small clearing. The house that comes into view as they approach is by far the biggest shock they've had *all* day.

You could say it's white? Mostly. At least, when you consider the paint that is still attached and not peeling. The windows are boarded up, and the gingerbread lattice is only intact on one side of the second-story balcony. At the very top is another large window, indicating possibly an attic of sorts. It's the only window that's been left untouched. This decrepit, quite possibly condemned, Victorian-style house is to be their new residence.

Eve's mouth drops open.

Not blinking, the car idles as they sit gaping, unwilling to leave the safety of their car just yet.

Shock.

When Jill had said they would have a free place to live, this wasn't what Eve had in mind.

"No...I swear, if you make me get out of this car, I will cut up all your precious little books while you are sleeping! Did you *not* ask Jill to send you any pictures?" Maggie screeches, her cheeks as red as her locks.

Too stunned to speak, Eve notices a second home set farther back to their right. Another two-story, white, run-down Victorian. They must have been built at the same time, at some point in the distant past. Architecturally, both structures are identical and currently competing in their state of disrepair.

Both buildings have been abandoned and forgotten, and maybe they should stay that way. A massive fallen branch blocks the second driveway, daring anyone to venture closer.

"Absolutely not." White as a ghost, Maggie sits, rigid, close to a state of panic. Or fainting. Or punching Eve, hard. Likely all three.

"Eve, I am going to turn around right now. We cannot...no, we *will* not be living here!" By the time she finishes her sentence, she's yelling.

The eldest Abbott secretly agrees, but they've reached a point of no return.

Jill said she had the water and power turned back on. So maybe this structure is more appealing on the inside? Maybe Jill installed the boards on the windows to prevent squatters? There has to be a reasonable explanation.

Gathering her courage, Eve ignores Maggie's protests and gets out. A cool breeze causes her to shiver as she folds her cardigan across her chest, using the belt to tie it closed. It takes all of her willpower to get her legs to cooperate. The cracked taillights cast an eerie glow onto the dirt road as Eve pops open the rusty back end. Locating a pillow, backpack, and sleeping bag, she closes it once more.

Frantically cranking her window down, Maggie leans out, her voice an octave higher when she yells, "What are you doing?"

"What does it look like I am doing? Grab your stuff."

Fishing the odd keychain out of her pocket, Eve studies it, waiting a moment for Maggie to join her. When she doesn't, Eve sighs and heads toward the front door on her own.

"You are freaking nuts, Eve! Come back here! Eve? Oh my God, you can't be serious!"

Relenting, Maggie also gets out and runs to grab a large bag and pillow from the backend, slamming it closed. Hurrying to the driver's side and swearing the entire time, she takes out the keys and turns off the headlights as Eve switches on the flashlight on her phone.

From the house. The other house. The forgotten house across the way, the closed curtains from a second-floor window part ever so slightly.

A black-gloved hand holds the moth-eaten fabric open, just enough.

It watches as the shadowed figures of two women shine thin lights through the night air, hurrying up the steps.

It knows them.

Eve and Maggie Abbott, daughters of Adel and Orion.

They should have never come.

The black gloved hand tightens its grip.

They will meet soon enough. And when they do, everything will change.

Chapter 4

The aged door groans with displeasure as Eve pushes it open, shining her phone's flashlight through the doorway. Particles that have been disturbed by their intrusion float through the air like a fog, only adding to the house's already-ominous nature. She tilts her light to the floor, spotting multiple footprints through the grime. Thankfully, the prints look to be about Jill's in size.

Their aunt may be an excellent cook, but it is evident that she is horrible at cleaning. Or maybe she wanted to get in, and out of, this space as quickly as possible?

If Eve asked the spiders who have turned the rafters into their webbed domain, they would probably tell her that no one had called this "home" in a very long time.

Both sisters cautiously step into the large living room. After they have cleared the frame, Maggie reluctantly forces the creaking door shut, locates a deadbolt, and turns it with a thud.

"Do you see any light switches?" Eve asks, scanning the room with her limited eyesight.

"I only see a bad decision...." Maggie groans.

"Stop complaining and start looking!" her older sister snaps, moving forward into the middle of the room. Huffing, Maggie does as she is asked, attempting to track one down herself.

This dwelling, at one time, must have been lovely. The bones of it are—the tall ceiling and thick, dark wood floors. Decorative crown molding separates the walls from the ceiling. Looking to the expansive, now-boarded-up windows, they must have let in a ton of light.

The room is empty, save for a substantial brick fireplace to their left, a built-in bookshelf with what appears to be a small jewelry box, and a chewed-up vintage sofa. Their footsteps echo, reverberating in the hollow space. Weathered floorboards squeak and crack with every stride.

"At least we won't have to install a security system? Even a ninja couldn't cross these floors undetected!" Maggie smirks, shining her light in Eve's face and temporarily blinding her.

"Would you stop?" she grumbles, awkwardly swatting at Maggie while still holding all her necessities from the car.

They continue to track down the elusive light switches with no luck. During one of their various phone calls, Jill had said that the power had been turned on prior to Eve and Maggie's arrival. Eve remembers her stating this clearly. It is odd that a house like this would have modern amenities, like plumbing, electricity, and running water. But their grandmother had lived here until four years ago. She must have made some improvements. Right?

Wallpaper, sporting blue and white flowers, is barely clinging to the walls, in some places folded down in half, no longer able to hold on to the exposed wood paneling.

"If we are in a horror movie right now, tag, you're the first one to die...." Maggie mutters, her voice croaking.

"Let's reserve judgment until morning. Who knows, we might be able to fix it up?" The lack of conviction in Eve's words betrayed her.

"Eve, dear, this house should be condemned. Bulldoze her down. Light her on fire. Who cares how you do it, but it needs to be done," she insists, her tone mocking but serious.

Maggie is probably right. But she also isn't naive. She begrudgingly knows that this house, and this town, is the last option from a long list of alternatives they have already exhausted.

Ignoring Maggie, Eve points her phone to the left, revealing a kitchen. Old cabinets, some with the doors partly or completely missing. Next, a retro refrigerator partially hidden by a stained butcher block in the center. Then a rusty wood-burning stove. Everything in this place is out of date, out of style, or out of commission.

Panning her phone to the right, Eve stops.

There is a man right in front of her, his black hair slicked back and large sharp fangs extended.

A vampire.

Eve, startled, screams bloody murder, dropping her phone. She turns to grab her sister and escape but freezes as a large chandelier hanging from the ceiling fills the room with light. Maggie is next to the entrance wall, having found the switch.

Pale, eyes wide, Maggie jumps as she sees the creature behind her older sister.

Then she snorts.

Laughing loudly and uncontrollably, Maggie points to the thing located behind Eve. Thinking her younger sister is under a spell, Eve whips around, only to get a good look at her assailant.

A cutout. A life-size cardboard cutout of Count Dracula is situated right in front of the stairs, sporting a yellow sticky note. It reads, "wet paint on railings" in Jill's distinct scrawl.

"I take it back. This house is awesome!" Maggie wheezes, clapping her hands together.

"Oh my God, that was terrifying...." Eve exhales, crossing her arms over her stomach. In part because she is suddenly freezing, and in part trying to hide the fact that she's shaking.

With the lights finally on, they both have a better view of the interior. Yes, it needs work, but it is obvious that Jill has been trying to spruce it up after hours. Paint cans with various used brushes and rollers are lined up below the banister.

On the lower level are the living room, kitchen, and two other rooms situated on either side of the staircase. Taking the lead once more, Maggie explores the first room, on the left. Yelling from the interior, her voice echoes, "Nothing in here but rusty nails and tetanus!"

Maggie joins Eve as she explores the second room, on the right, obviously being used for storage. Various boxes seem to be situated in a semi-circle, avoiding contact with a large, brownish-red stain on the flooring.

"Does that...?" Maggie doesn't finish her sentence before her sister interjects.

"It does."

"Not just me?"

"Nope."

"Does that smell like...?"

"Metallic? Yup."

"Do you think this is where grandma kicked the can?" stepping back, Maggie wrinkles her nose in disgust. She continues, "Do you think if we asked Jill, she would give us a straight answer?"

"Maggie, that's horrible!" Eve exclaims.

"She was murdered, Eve. Blood. Carpet. All that is missing is a chalk outline and some 'keep out' tape," Maggie says casually.

"Never coming in here again…." Eve mutters, quickly exiting the room. Maggie shuts the door and follows.

They edge around Dracula and make their way up to the second floor. Two doors again, leading to two rooms on either side. Choosing left first, they're pleasantly surprised when it reveals a decent sized bathroom with a clawfoot tub-shower combo, checkerboard subway tile, a sink with an etched mirror above it, and antique light fixtures. It was actually…cute.

"Do you think Grandma was remodeling and ran out of money? Because this ain't half bad!" Maggie throws down her backpack on the charming floor. Unzipping, she pulls out a toiletry bag, toothbrush, and toothpaste. Retrieving a hair tie as well, she arranges her curls into a messy bun. Maggie then leans over the sink, locates the hot and cold, and turns the "hot" knob on full. Flicking her fingers through the running water, she tests for the right temperature.

"What? Are you gonna watch?" Maggie asks, squeezing toothpaste onto the bristles and plopping it in her mouth as Eve stands in the doorway.

"You don't want to see the rest of the house?" the eldest Abbott sister inquires, stumped.

"Nope, I'm sleeping in the bathroom."

Eve knows that Maggie is more than likely serious.

"Suit yourself." Trying to sound confident, Eve backs away from the door, secretly wishing that Maggie hadn't dismissed her and forced her to continue on her own. Taking a few steps, she notices rose-covered wallpaper, cream and pink this time. Still peeling and in disrepair, it has a certain sort of charm. The floors are the same style and shape as below, but they don't crack and pop with every step. Locating another light switch next to a ladder, she flips it on. Looking up, there is a ladder that leads to a trap door—more than likely an attic. Deciding to explore the room on the right first, she's instantly glad she did.

Turning a dimmer knob near the entrance, another chandelier illuminates an almost-empty bedroom. This room—this room is Eve's. In the middle of the back wall is a large bay window, and a pillow-less reading nook. Once the outside boards are removed, the panes of glass will fill the space with warm sunlight during the day. Hugging the window on either side are recessed shelves that will be perfect for her treasured literature. Taking a deep breath, Eve lets it out, sending it up to the high ceiling, framed by intricate floral crown molding.

She feels like she's in something out of a fairy tale.

A new cast-iron bed with soft-looking pillows and blankets sits against the wall to the left. Fully expecting to have to spend the night in the sleeping bag she brought with her, Eve could cry.

Jill. This has to be Jill.

And then there's a scream.

Maggie.

Startled, Eve drops her things and runs out into the hallway. Seeing light coming through the now-open trap door in the ceiling, she frantically climbs the ladder, sticking her head through the square opening. Spotting Maggie, she is surprised to see the massive smile plastered on her sister's face.

"Dibs! Dibs! I call dibs!" Maggie squeals, twirling in the center of the room.

A vaulted ceiling with exposed beams frames two large glass windows on either end of the room. In the center, against the wall, another cast iron bed and bedding, duplicate to the one below. How Jill had gotten this bed into this room, and through that crawl space, is beyond Eve.

Large metal sconces gleam, providing soft lighting.

Climbing the rest of the way into the attic, Eve plops on to the floor, breathing labored.

"Do you think we could put in another bathroom and, like, a kitchenette up here? Maybe add a set of stairs from the outside? Because then I could just shut this door and never have to see you!"

Noticing the hurt look on Eve's face, Maggie sobers. Biting her nails, she's quiet for a moment before marching over to Eve and joining her on the floor. Scooting next to her, she leans her head on her older sister's shoulder.

"I think I'm going to like it here," she whispers in her ear.

"Me too."

Eve wonders if she means it. If she will ever feel safe here, and if this home will really be just that—a home.

Or if maybe her instincts earlier were right—in that alleyway, when every fiber of her being was telling her to run.

Chapter 5

Jill gives the Abbotts a week to settle in. After that point, Eve will be required at the café, and Maggie will be just in time to start her fall semester at Saintsville High. Both girls have seven days of freedom until they will be locked down with obligations.

Honestly, the girls wish that they could take the time to relax and explore, having already traveled so far, but making their new dwelling habitable is priority number one.

And that priority is turning out to be way more than they bargained for.

On their first morning, they decide it best to tackle the kitchen. Thankfully, the old blue 1950s refrigerator works, minus the arctic temperatures blasting anyone who dares open the freezer.

Eve struggles, her cleaning towels already stained black from the counters. She doesn't seem to be removing the dirt, just spreading it around, leaving muddy lines on the marble, further complicated by the clogged sink and a lack of a washer or dryer on the premises. The Abbotts will have no choice but to frequent the laundromat next to the market in town.

Their aunt left them some milk and dried cereal, but after breakfast, they're going to be on their own. Eve adds groceries to their many things to do that day, and if they want to eat anything hot, tackling the wood-burning stove is a must.

Maggie jumps at the chance to hit anything with an ax, and being the more coordinated one, offers to chop some wood for their future meals. A natural, she has a decent pile stacked against the house in no time.

Brushing her curls away from the sweat beading on her forehead, she gives the ax one last swing, lodging it back into the stump where she found it. Looking up and into the woods, she stops. From a distance, deep within the tightly spaced trees, she swears she sees something.

A shadow.

Tall, and dark, maybe belonging to a man? She blinks, and whatever or whoever it was is gone.

Without hesitation, she wrenches the ax from the stump and raises it, lowering it slowly over her right shoulder. Gripping the handle tightly with both hands, she is ready to swing. Maggie turns her body to the side, making herself smaller as she takes on a defensive posture. Feeling somewhat safer with a weapon, she scans the woods.

But with a loud screech, the back door of the old house opens.

Startled, Maggie whips her head around, eyes ablaze.

"Maggie?" Eve questions, her smile falling.

"I'm not making you clean, no need to chop me up," Eve teases, confused.

Maggie doesn't respond, turning her head back to the forest.

"What is it?" Eve speaks again, her concern growing.

There's a pause before Maggie slowly lowers the ax. Making some unspoken decision, she turns and walks slowly over to Eve.

"I saw something. Must have been an animal," she grumbles.

Not wanting to sound ridiculous, Maggie keeps what she thinks she saw to herself. They're living in the wilderness after all, and more than likely sharing their surroundings with a multitude of wildlife.

"I'm heading into town before everything closes. Want to join?" Eve inquires.

"Uh-huh," Maggie agrees, scanning the forest once more.

Having her answer, Eve retreats back indoors, probably to find her purse and keys as Maggie walks over to the stump, intending on returning the ax to where she had found it. Tilting her eyes to the woods, nothing is amiss, but something tells her to keep it close. Maggie carries the ax with her as she walks to the house, up the stairs, and inside.

Just in case.

Day two is uneventful. They find a tall folding ladder and evict as many spiders as possible. Maggie is unusually sober as she works beside her sister. Eve just chalks her silence up to ghosts. Not literal ghosts, but the ghosts of their lives thus far. Being here was bound to be triggering, and taking Maggie away from everything she has ever known even more so.

While dusting in the boarded-up living room, Eve notices the small jewelry box she had forgotten about on their first night. Wiping it off with a rag, she carries it back into the center of the room. Sitting carefully on the old couch—now draped with a painting drop cloth—she cracks open the lid and is puzzled by its contents.

Purple velvet lining displays a small silver necklace. Removing it from the box, Eve sees the chain is long, at least thirty inches, but the round pendant is odd. Circular in shape, simple, the center looks to be transparent. Almost like a magnifying glass, but this glass has an iridescent quality as she tilts it back and forth, catching the light shining down from the chandelier.

"Whatcha got there?" Maggie mumbles, curious and leaning over Eve's shoulder. Before Maggie has a chance to claim it as hers, Eve throws the necklace on, raising the pendant to eye level.

"Cool," Maggie shrugs. "It's yours. I would be creeped out wearing something that belonged to Grandma, anyways. She'll probably haunt you for it."

Relieved to see Maggie in a better mood, Eve relaxes.

"Ha, ha. If she does, at least we know she isn't an evil spirit."

Setting her hammer down, Maggie grabs an apple from the fridge and plops next to Eve on the couch. *Crunch.* Taking a big bite, she leans back, lost in thought.

"But don't you think it's weird? Grandma is killed one month before our parents disappear? For all we know, she could have died on this very couch. Something is hella fishy...."

Another crunch as Maggie takes another big bite, unfazed.

"I did try asking Jill about it—"

"And?" Maggie interrupts.

"Anytime I bring up June, she changes the subject."

"Yet another reason not to trust her." Giving Eve a knowing look, Maggie gets up and grabs her hammer.

Eve protectively tucks the necklace under her shirt.

The sisters work outside from midday to dusk. Removing the nailed boards from the windows on the lower level, one by one.

As they do, they are mystified. All of the panes of glass underneath are fully intact, so the boards weren't installed because of repair. There really wasn't anything in the house to steal, so they definitely weren't put in place for protection. Saintsville is devoid of tornados or any sort of natural disasters that would require precautions like this. Maybe this had just been Jill's way of grieving?

Unable to finish with the second level without borrowing a larger ladder from Jill, they have made almost an entire loop around the house. With one window left, Maggie and Eve tug on the nails with their hammers as they hear a rumbling in the distance.

The sound is coming from down the road, as a dirt cloud moves steadily closer. She hears the roaring as two automobiles—a black muscle car and a generic moving truck—come into view.

"Did you order furniture?" a puzzled Maggie inquires, turning to Eve for answers.

"Nope."

"Interesting…."

The solid black hot rod heads straight toward them, but veers right, passing their parked station wagon. It comes to a stop in front of the large fallen tree, the one blocking the driveway to the other forgotten home. The moving van slows to a halt, idling a hundred or so feet back, giving the sleek black car room to work.

From the driver's side exits the first figure. A man, wearing back aviators, a black tank top, black pants, and black combat boots with his head shaved. Muscular arms are covered in tattoos, too hard to make out from a distance, but from their vantage point at the window, Eve thinks they look like lines. Bar codes. Whoever he is, he is breathtaking.

As if on cue, three more males emerge—all covered in the same odd markings. They have to be related, though their personal styles vary. The second male's head is shaved, like the first, but sports glasses like Eve. He seems to be giving instructions to the other two that appear from the passenger-side door, while the first male stands with his arms crossed, waiting.

The third maybe-brother has a nose ring, only half his head shaved, and the other half encompassed by complex braids. And the fourth, who looks to be about Maggie's age, is sporting a black beanie…covering up whatever hair he does or doesn't have.

The Abbott sisters stand, mouths agape.

Is this some kind of joke?

Two by two, the boys split, heading to the sports car's trunk as it pops open. From within, they start to pull out long, thick silver chains.

"What are they doing?" Maggie whispers, not wanting to be discovered just yet, too enthralled by the beautiful creatures before her.

"I think they're going to try and move that tree…." Eve states, also transfixed. Where Maggie is excited by the attractive male prospects, Eve grimaces.

"Who are they?" states Maggie seductively. Based on how she purrs those three words, Eve knows that trouble will soon follow.

"I think…they're our new neighbors."

Chapter 6

Are they brothers? That is yet to be discovered. Whoever they are, they work quickly. Three lift the tree on the left end, while one throws a chain underneath, and they repeat this on the right side as well, bringing it over the top of the weathered pine and securing it. The male with the half-shaved head and braids, and the one with a beanie, carry the two ends of chain to meet, forming a sort of triangle with the fallen log. Unhooking a winch from the hot rod, the guy with glasses now drags a metal cable forward as the Abbotts continue to stare. He deftly slides the ends of the chains onto a large hook attached to the winch and backs away.

All of this takes them, maybe, five minutes? They don't converse while they set about their task, just move and flow, effortlessly, as one unit.

"This is, by far, the hottest thing I have ever seen...." Maggie declares earnestly.

"Do you think they're some sort of cult?" Eve whispers, just in case they can possibly hear her.

"If they are, I have found my true calling!" Maggie drops her hammer and leans back against the house. Quickly unbuttoning the bottom three or four snaps on her flannel, she ties it, exposing her midriff.

"Really?" Eve scolds, hoping to chastise her sister into covering up. "Why stop there? Why not take off your entire top?"

"I want one of them to...."

"Maggie!" Louder than she meant to, Eve yells her little sister's name.

Both girls turn back toward "operation tree," and all four of the males have stopped moving and are looking straight at them. The half-shaved, glasses, and youngest have moved out of the way, giving the oldest brother clearance. He's about to get back into the black car but is angled toward Eve. His stance is powerful and menacing—muscles tense and corded, as if he could pounce at any moment.

Eve turns cold. Whoever these people are, she knows one thing for sure. They are dangerous.

"Really?! Why do you always have to embarrass me?" Maggie whispers, covering her face with her gloved hands.

Eve sheepishly waves hello and the strangers relax, but they don't return the gesture. Instead, they turn their attention once again to the fallen tree.

Her cheeks heat, doubly embarrassed by their dismissal. Not waiting for Maggie, Eve ferociously attacks another nail, ripping it free from the board. Maggie soon picks up her hammer and joins her sister, but both women are still very much aware of the new arrivals.

"Who keeps chains like that in their car? Unless they knew they were going to need them?" Eve whispers.

"They obviously knew they were going to need them, or how else were they going to move that tree—levitation?" Maggie snarks.

"This is too weird...."

"*You're* weird. You can leave, and they can most definitely stay!"

The black hot rod roars to life, catching the sisters' attention once more. Eve assumes the oldest male is driving as he throws it into gear, hits the gas, and a loud crack emits as the pine starts to shift. The tires, spitting out dirt, dig in and force the car forwards with the tree in tow. Swinging around, the pine is pulled off the road to the left. Once the blockage has been cleared, the other three outside of the car spring into action. Removing the chain, stowing the winch, and joining the patriarch of their group back in their vehicle. Thrown into drive again, the sports car rips down the driveway with the moving truck following closely behind.

"Do you think we should go say hi?" Maggie asks hopefully, but Eve just groans.

"We have two more windows to go."

"Buzzkill."

"Let them get settled in," Eve states reasonably. "I'm sure we will find out more about them soon enough."

The girls finish the last lower-level window just before sundown and head inside. The boys have parked, headed indoors, and haven't revealed themselves since. No lights on, either—their newly inhabited house is pitch black.

Day three, the Abbott sisters are awoken by a chainsaw.

Eve drowsily throws on her glasses and hobbles to her window to pinpoint the source of the noise. Peeking through the cracks over her still-boarded window—they really need to locate a taller ladder soon—she sees the shaved head and notes it to be the angry driver from the day prior.

And he is topless.

Sporting the same black pants and combat boots, sans shirt, she sees that the barcode-like tattoos cover most of his chiseled upper body, and head south. Eve wonders just how far down the tattoos extend when she hears a thud above her. Maggie must have been woken by the noise as well.

Locating her cellphone and unplugging it from its charger, she sees the time is 6:30 a.m.

From the attic, Eve hears her baby sister yawn loudly, squeal, pounding as she runs, then her voice shouting down the ladder, "Eve? Get up here!" *Thump, thump, thump* as Maggie sprints back over her head, more than likely to the large vaulted window facing toward the front of the house.

Putting on a fuzzy gray bathrobe and slippers, Eve patters out of her room and up the ladder, entering Maggie's space. Spotting her little sister, she grins. Her wild curls are especially voluminous this morning. Hair sticking up at odd angles, the petite redhead looks like she is five years old again, minus the missing teeth and with curves. With a blanket wrapped around her, she waves and beckons for Eve to join her.

"This is better than cable." Maggie snorts, turning back to the window.

They're surprised to see five males, not four, hard at work. The fifth must have been driving the moving truck; his short blonde hair is spiked. They all seem to have assigned tasks. Clearing debris, what looks to be parts of rusted old cars and barrels. The male who they assume is the youngest Eve almost doesn't recognize at first without the beanie, but his shoulder-length locks are now held back by a black bandana. He's setting markers—little metal flags that he seems to be laser measuring. Every ten feet along the border of their property, another orange marker gets pushed into the ground.

"Please tell me they are putting in an outdoor gym! Do you have any binoculars?"

Laughing, Eve responds, "No."

"Well, I *am* seventeen in a few months. Consider it an early birthday present?"

Actually, Eve doesn't consider binoculars to be such a bad idea. She wouldn't mind getting a closer look. More to spy on the suspicious figures, and follow their movements, of course. At least that's what she is telling herself. This home only needs one boy-crazed female.

"I'll think about it...." Kissing Maggie's head, Eve stretches, and heads back downstairs to make breakfast.

Days four, five, six, and seven turn into a blur of cleaning, painting, and more spying. The brothers, in four days, have completely clear cut the field, dug ditches, and installed tall posts. Even more odd, at the top of each post are massive light panels. Not facing toward their abode but turned toward Eve and Maggie's. From what they could tell, gawking from the attic window, not one attempt has been made on home improvements. Just the field. And the lights. That seemed to be their main focus.

The Abbotts' seven-day respite has come to an end. It is Monday, which means Eve's first day working at Jill's, and Maggie's first day as a high school junior. So far, the day is off to a rough start. The wiring in the kitchen can't be up to code, as the toaster starts sparking and burns two slices of bread to a crisp. Switching gears, Eve quickly grabs two more pieces of multi-grain and slaps on some peanut butter and honey. That will have to do for breakfast, as they are already running late.

The eldest Abbott has woken up early enough, taken time to tie her hair back into a chic bun, and even applied minimal makeup. Nervous, Eve is unsure what the dress code for her new job entails. Settling on a simple, navy-blue dress and cream ballet flats, she thought it said, "I work at a café."

Entering the kitchen, Maggie has also apparently put in her own unique sort of effort to get ready. Her normally wild ringlets are split into two French braids. Sporting a cut-off band shirt, jeans, and sneakers, she is effortlessly cool, like always. Completing her look is a hooded sweatshirt tied around her waist, which Eve wishes her sister would just wear, but she knows better than to say anything.

Maggie has on maybe a bit too much eye makeup as well, in Eve's opinion. A smokey pink shadow and black winged liner only magnify the intensity of her gorgeous blue eyes.

Checking her phone, Eve groans. Throwing the unplugged toaster in the sink and handing her sister a paper towel with one slice of bread, she grabs the other, her purse and keys, and rushes toward the front door.

"Maggie, backpack, let's go!"

"Don't tell me, you really got a job at my school…."

"What?"

"You look like a librarian," Maggie snorts.

Holding the front door open with her foot, Eve motions toward the car, used to Maggie's insults. She watches as her younger sister sets down her breakfast and unhurriedly retrieves a water bottle from the fridge.

"*Now*, Mags! I'll meet you in the car!"

Eve takes a bite of her toast as she power walks to the station wagon. Minutes pass and Maggie has still not come out. Honking the horn, she finally sees her emerge with her backpack in one hand and honeyed bread in the other, but she still manages to flip Eve the bird. Locking the front door, she stows her keys in her backpack and casually strolls to the car.

Finally in the automobile, Maggie's door isn't even shut before Eve guns it.

"What the hell!" Maggie exclaims, setting her napkin and partially eaten breakfast on the dash, swinging the passenger side door shut, and firmly clicking her seatbelt into place.

"If you aren't ready to leave the house by seven thirty tomorrow, I swear, you're walking!"

Eve is on edge. There are just too many unanswered questions in her life at the moment.

What happened to their grandmother?

What happened to their parents?

Is their current living situation safe?

Can she trust Jill?

Who the heck are the strangers holed up in the house across the field?

And now, one more question.

Why could she see their sleek, black hot rod approaching in her rearview mirror?

"You have to be kidding...." Eve grimaces, not ready at all for what this particular day might bring.

Chapter 7

Every turn Eve makes, the hot rod follows. As it tails them through town, it becomes increasingly evident that both cars are headed in the direction of the high school. Oblivious, Maggie chatters away. She is nervous, although she would never admit it. Back in Seattle, Maggie had a solid group of friends. Girls and guys she had befriended from preschool up. She fit in, knew her place, and quite frankly, was queen bee.

And now she's the new girl.

In this town, Maggie already knows she doesn't belong. The looks she has received every time they venture to the market, or hardware store...well, they aren't warm and friendly. The residents of this anomaly are aloof, calculating, and wary. Maggie highly doubts anyone here listens to indie rock or stays out past their curfew. Saintsville doesn't like edgy newcomers. She can tell by the judgmental stares of mothers and fathers, as if she might corrupt their children. And honestly, they are probably right to worry. Maggie has always done what she wanted, when she wanted, with whomever she wanted. But all she wants, in this moment, is to blink and wake up in her former life.

Normally Eve is pretty empathic. Attuned to her sister's moods, she should see that Maggie is on edge. That her—not so little anymore—sister is hurting. That in this moment, she really needs her.

But Eve is currently preoccupied by the two predatory males currently tailgating their beat-up ride. From what she can garner, the shaved-head, chainsaw-wielding, yet-to-be named older brother is once again driving. He always seems to be driving, which Eve attributes to him needing to be in control. Or it's his car, and he's horrible at sharing. On the passenger side sits the long-haired teenager. Eve's worst suspicious are confirmed when they finally reach Saintsville High, and the distinct black sports car is firmly behind them in the drop-off queue.

"No…you can't be serious?" Eve mumbles to herself, staring in the rearview mirror.

"What?" Maggie asks, checking her makeup in a small compact.

"Nothing…."

"What? What's wrong?"

Noticing that Eve's focus seems to be on what's behind them, Maggie whips around, sees their neighbor's car, and gasps.

"Fuck yeah!" Maggie exclaims, winking at Eve.

"You know our windows aren't tinted," Eve points out. "They can see you right now."

"Let them look…."

Maggie leans on the seat back, flashing a seductive smile.

From within the other car, Maggie watches as the younger male's mouth turns up ever so slightly.

He is smiling too.

There is absolutely nothing impressive about this school. Located smack dab in the middle of two farms, it's oddly out of place. There are cornfields on either side, and a large, square, pink stone building. There are also a few—also pink—smaller buildings hugging a football field. Realizing that, apparently, the school's mascot is an angel—Saintsville, *Saints*—Maggie guesses it makes sense. A terrifying, biblical-looking man with large wings is painted on the outside of the main entry.

Judging every soul that enters.

Probably judging her pink eyeshadow, which she now regrets wearing.

The parking lot could hold maybe fifty cars, max. But as the students pour off the typical yellow bus, Maggie is led to believe that a lot of her peers choose not to drive. Or, more than likely, their uptight parents don't let them. Eve had floored it the moment Maggie had gotten out, abandoning the teenager to her fate.

God forbid Eve wasn't twenty minutes early to her first day at Jill's.

Eve. Maggie always associates her sister with a puzzle. Too many pieces, and too many unturned.

Maggie wonders if maybe her sister just needs to acquire a social life? If Eve actually had some friends, then maybe she wouldn't be on Maggie's back so much. Even a little romance could do her good, but Maggie has no clue what her sister is into. For all she knows, Eve could be a lesbian.

No judgment there. Maggie is known for being fluid, appreciating beauty regardless of her latest infatuation's gender. But Eve hadn't gone on a date, had a crush, or hooked up with anyone since their parents' disappearance, male or female. At least not to Maggie's knowledge. And now, there were five of the hottest male specimens Maggie had ever seen in her life, living right next door to them, and Eve was treating the beefcakes like they were lepers. Or cavemen? Neanderthals who were going to club Maggie and Eve and drag them by their hair back to their cave.

Not that Maggie would object.

And she knows, without turning around, that one of the five is somewhere behind her.

Maggie's stomach tingles in excitement, hoping beyond hope that whoever he is, he will be in one of her classes.

First period, according to the crumpled piece of paper she holds, is English. She already has her class schedule memorized, but holding it gives her something to do with her hands. Heading up the steps, she enters and locates her locker. A nerdy yearbook guy—Phil? Paul? Something with a *P*—gave her a tour last week. It was the only time Eve let her leave the house since their arrival, besides grocery runs, the laundromat, or random errands.

His upper lip was sweaty, dressed in a checkered wool sweater and tan khakis, but that was all that Maggie really remembered. She had taken one look at his pants and burned his existence from her memory.

Looking down the main hallway, her worst fears are confirmed.

This school is too dang small. Phil-Paul told her that her arrival was very exciting, as they haven't had a "new kid" in over a year. At least Eve was right about one thing. Saintsville did have more than 140 residents. Fifty years had passed since their town sign had been erected on the highway, and now they were up to a whopping 353. Amazing what you can find out when you're bored and have Wi-Fi.

Apparently, students from a neighboring town were bused in as well. So in total, the high school had a roster of around a hundred between all four grades.

Thirty of those students being football players.

So cliché. Small town. Football is king. Maggie feels like she is trapped in an episode of *Friday Night Lights*.

Also apparently, Maggie is the only person here with a sense of style. Minus her mysteriously sexy neighbor.

The girls are mostly wearing knee-length dresses. Or jeans and flowy floral tops. Their hair perfectly styled. Makeup, soft and dewy. Virginal.

Maggie could vomit.

Looking at the various bodies as she walks, there are a few that vary from the status quo. Like any school, there is a smattering of nerds and attention seekers. But for the most part, Maggie likens the females to wannabe beauty queens. And the males—button-down shirts with a clean-cut vibe. Lots of letterman jackets and hair gel. She doesn't mind them as much, as they are wholesome and ripe for debauchery.

All eyes are on Maggie as she makes her way down the hall.

The more heads that turn—the more that people whisper, pointing straight at her—the more defiant she feels.

Fine. If they want to stare, she is going to give them something to stare at.

Passing a pretty blonde, with stick-straight shiny hair, Maggie can see that she is mid-laugh. Touching the arm of the jock in front of her, his crooked smile indicating that he is enjoying her advances. If Maggie had to guess, this female is popular. Spoiled, by the looks of her designer handbag and expensive clothing, a rarity in these parts. Maggie groans internally, knowing already that she and this girl are going to clash.

Noticing Maggie, the freckled, wavy-haired, crooked-smile, letterman-jacket-sporting jock stops talking midsentence.

Suddenly, the blonde no longer exists.

Wondering what on earth could be so important, the popular girl locates the new girl, and instantly, she knows who has stolen her spotlight. Eyes narrowing, she scowls.

It is almost as if Maggie can read the thoughts running through the blonde's head. That she is a goth, or "alternative." Someone new for her and her followers to gossip about. Maggie has only been at school for a few minutes, and already made her first enemy.

Making matters worse, Maggie purposely locks eyes with the object of the blonde's attention and flashes him a dazzling smile, passing them both. Taking a quick left, she locates the classroom for her first period. Once inside, Maggie's relieved to find it empty.

Heading straight to the back, she chooses a desk in the far-left corner. Not that there are many options, with the max capacity of the room at roughly twenty. Taking out her cracked cellphone, she puts in her ear buds, trying to drown out her agitation. Maggie usually likes attention, but that had been too much, even for her.

Technically, she knows that cellphones are to be off except for lunch—she had lazily read through the classroom rules in her welcome packet, and that particular policy had stood out. But she highly doubts that she will be doled out detention on her first day.

In her hallway escape, she has forgotten about the guy living in the house across the field. One of the five she's been secretly watching this past week.

That is, until a pair of black leather boots come into view.

And she looks up.

Eve looks up from the scalding coffee spilled on the floor and grinds her teeth. She's worked as a barista before. In the language of latte and cappuccino she is fluent. But Jill's espresso machine, which she fondly calls "Bertha," well...Eve is convinced that her aunt's apparatus is possessed. The hot water tap works for Jill, but when Eve tries it, the water is ice cold. Don't even start Eve on the steam wand, which is already responsible for multiple burns, including the coffee spill that just occurred.

She wants to quit and it's only her first day.

A plump man with a receding hairline and a rosy face waits patiently. He reminds Eve of Santa Claus, sans beard. Eve, mopping up the floor with a rag, notices him rocking back and forth on his toes. The poor man has been waiting over ten minutes, and Eve has yet to deliver him his hot mocha.

"Hey, Mister Mayor. How are you on this fine Monday?" Jill, coming from the back, looks adorable in her red-and-white-striped apron, a splash of baking flour on one cheek. Her messy, Maggie-like curls are piled on top of her head as Jill continues to greet their other customers by name.

Noticing her aunt, the Mayor's already-red cheeks deepen.

So far, during the hour that Eve has been working behind the counter, it seems that every customer who enters is courting her aunt. No wonder she has such a thriving business. Not an easy feat in this sleepy town, when most customers have easily a thirty-minute commute just for a scone and a cup of joe.

Noticing her niece in distress and knowing the Mayor's usual, Jill swiftly whips up his mocha and hands it over. Disappointed that their interlude is over, the Mayor leaves, indicated by the bells on the doors chiming as he exits. Eve is on her hands and knees, scrubbing. The pile of towels at her side are thoroughly soaked.

"Honey, you need to show Bertha who's boss. She's a mean old bat, but I swear, this girl makes the best espresso.... Those new machines don't come close!" she insists, patting Bertha fondly.

Eve suppresses the urge to look at her aunt like she is insane. "I am so sorry, I'm trying!"

"Don't worry love, I'm going to go grab you a few more towels!" Jill offers with a warm smile. She heads into the back, leaving Eve to her misery.

Chime. The door opens. The sound of multiple pairs of boots on the linoleum forces Eve to look up.

Through the glass bakery case, she sees them.

Four tall, tattooed, muscular, now-familiar faces.

The neighbors.

Chapter 8

Shooting straight to her feet, Eve's eyes are wide. She looks toward the back room, willing Jill to hurry back with the extra linens. Maybe she can make some excuse, head to the restroom, and hide until they leave?

Anything to avoid interacting with...them.

Eve's sleek bun from that morning is now lopsided, pieces of loose hair hanging down around the bangs framing her face. The foam from the failed mocha is splattered throughout her locks, marring her simple dress as well. The four men approach, with the one with half his head closely shaved and braids taking the lead.

Eve definitely doesn't like the way he's looking at her.

Studying the menu for a moment, he then leans across the counter, closing the uncomfortable distance between them. Her heart is pounding.

"Hi. Can we get four espressos? One a double shot?" His voice is gravelly and raspy. Provocative. "And your name? I believe you live next door, but we haven't been properly introduced."

Eve can't move. She knows she must look like an idiot, but try as she might, no words will come out her mouth. She and Maggie have spent the good part of the past week staring at these very humans, and now that they are right in front of her, she has no clue what to say.

"Okay, there are more in the drawer next to the knives if you need them…." Jill begins to explain, but she doesn't complete her sentence as she emerges from the kitchen holding a stack of towels. Her eyes narrow, spotting the threat before her.

This side of Jill Eve hasn't seen before. Her aunt turns cold. It's obvious that they know each other, and Eve's actually more terrified of Jill in this moment than the neighbors. Not looking at Eve, she tosses the rags onto the floor, the white fabric turning brown as they soak up her niece's many mistakes.

"Rowan…."

"This place hasn't changed much." The man—*is* his name Rowan?—plays with the tip jar, brushing off Jill's aggression.

"What do you want?" states Jill, moving to stand securely in front of Eve.

"Coffee."

"What do you really want?"

With this he laughs, the other three remaining silent in the background.

"I see you haven't changed. And who's the pretty girl behind you?"

Eve rolls her eyes, her fear lessening. Suddenly embarrassed by her cowardice, she moves to stand beside her aunt.

"Eve. I'm Eve. Jill, four espressos, one a double. I'll ring them up."

Weighing her options, Jill decides to make their drinks. The sooner she's done and they're gone, the better.

Now in front of the register, Eve presses the designated keys and accepts the cash handed to her. As she doles out his change, Rowan speaks again.

"Aren't you going to ask who I am?" Flirting, he leans further forward on the counter. Eve studies him for a moment. He's pale—all of them are—but it doesn't detract from his classic beauty. Chiseled cheeks, a full mouth and dark brown eyes. The blonde hair on the right side of his head is a combination of dreads and braids. Not readily apparent from their view from the attic had been the small metal charms woven throughout with care.

"Jill called you Rowan. So I assume you're Rowan...?" Eve suggests warily.

"Bingo. The one with the glasses is my brother Martin. The angry guy in the middle is Tate, and the serious one on the right is our family's firstborn, Luca. We, fair maiden, are the Quinns."

Anyone else calling her a "fair maiden" would have caused Eve to gag. But Rowan has a way of making every word he utters alluring.

So, Eve and Maggie were right. They are all brothers.

Taking a quick peek at the three behind Rowan, Eve is fascinated by their genetic similarities...but even more so by how much they differ. Martin seems shrewd, no-nonsense. His facial structure is akin to Rowan's, but his jaw is square. Intelligent, dark blue irises in contrast to Rowan's brown. She can tell, looking at Tate next, that he's the broken one. Blue, like Martin, but his eyes are cold and menacing. Of the four she has met so far, he worried her the most. Tate is bigger, more muscular than his brothers. Stocky in frame with a thick neck, he reminds Eve of an ape.

Lastly, locking eyes with Luca, her stomach flutters. He is the tallest of the bunch, his features more angled. Hawk-like.

Almond eyes—a warm caramel brown—are studying her. His gaze is so intense that Eve's cheeks flush, forcing her to look away.

Changing her mind, she decides that Luca is, by far, her biggest threat.

Slam. Four small paper cups make contact with the counter, causing Eve to flinch.

With a salute, Rowan grabs the espressos and retreats.

"Nice to see you, Jill. It's good to be home!"

Chapter 9

M aggie is positively giddy.

Looking up from her desk and into the face of the delicious young man before her, she's suddenly glad that they moved. She is thankful for the dilapidated shack they call home. She fully supports every decision made by Eve that brought her to this moment. Like that, like a switch being flipped, things are finally looking brighter.

If she would have known a month ago that male prospects like *this* existed? And that she would get the chance to try and seduce them? Her and her red curls would have bounced with joy all the way to Saintsville.

None of this shows externally, of course, as she calmly leans forward onto her desk and smirks.

Grinning back, he flashes his perfect white teeth. Deep dimples frame his full mouth. Up close, he's even more handsome than she thought. With his flawless skin and shoulder-length, wavy blonde hair, half of which he has tied back. The intensity in his light brown eyes is mesmerizing as he crouches down before her. Reaching under her desk, he picks up a pen from the floor and sets it in front of Maggie.

Taking out her headphones, she studies the generic ballpoint.

"Sorry, not mine," Maggie shrugs.

"It is now," he teases, sitting down in a seat beside her.

"But what if I don't want it?"

Picking up the writing device, Maggie places it on his desk. His eyebrows raise as he reaches for the pen, giving Maggie a chance to study him more. Staring at his exposed arms, Maggie can tell they are defined and muscular, covered in a complex pattern dominating the surface. To say his tattoos are unusual would be an understatement. In her experience, people's ink usually had a random aesthetic. Mermaids, skulls, sappy inspirational quotes, favorite cereals. They were either spontaneous, or extremely personal in nature.

The small thick lines with breaks in between, covering both of his arms, have no clear message. Angled various directions, they remind her of an intricate maze.

"It's not polite to return a gift," he prods with mock annoyance, setting the pen back in front of her.

"I don't accept gifts from strangers," Maggie taunts.

"We're not strangers."

"We've never met...."

He holds out his large hand, and Maggie accepts, giving it a shake.

"West."

"Maggie."

"So...you're the girl in the attic."

"Well...shit." Maggie mumbles, causing West to laugh.

If Maggie would have known that they could see her, she wouldn't have been so obvious in her reconnaissance. Neither she nor Eve had seen them look the direction of their shack once while they had been doing God knows what to that field. But West did seek her out today and is being straightforward about her spying. If he is creeped out by it, he isn't giving her any indication.

Maybe he is the voyeuristic type? She could work with that.

A high-pitched female voice pushes into their conversation, forcing West and Maggie to turn.

"You live in an attic? Wow...charming?"

Maggie can't help but groan, noticing the attractive blonde from the hallway planted firmly in front of them, her delicate features arranged in manufactured concern. Maggie hadn't even noticed the classroom filling up, the seats now half occupied.

She'd been too interested in West to care.

"I'm Zoe," says the pert blonde, to West only, gracefully seating herself in front of him. "You are...?" she continues.

"West," he mumbles politely, brushing her off.

Good. Maggie takes his dismissal as a cue to continue with their previous banter.

"You guys were the ones chopping, digging, and mowing all hours of the day," the youngest Abbott playfully accuses, her voice lowered.

From the corner of her eye, Maggie sees Zoe flip her hair in frustration, turning with a huff toward the chalkboard.

"Nosey neighbors are the worst," he teases.

"Really? I was going to say nosey blondes...." It's an obvious dig toward Zoe, which doesn't go unnoticed, her manicured nails digging into the desk's battered surface.

A loud bell rings, and their English teacher enters. He's older, near retirement if Maggie had to guess. Small in size with large glasses, salt-and-pepper hair, and a kind face. She thinks he says his name is Mr. Harris as he rattles off some sort of introduction, then instructs the students to take out a piece of paper.

Picking up her backpack from the concrete floor and unzipping it, she takes out a simple notebook and a floral pencil case.

West's hand touches her wrist, sending a strong shock straight up her arm.

"Ouch!" she whispers, rubbing her shoulder and giggling. It is obvious, in more ways than one, that they have a spark.

"Sorry… Can I borrow a piece of paper, and a pen?"

"You have to be kidding," Maggie states after a moment, realizing that West doesn't have any sort of backpack or supplies.

Taking *that* pen once again from her desk, Maggie leans across and firmly plants it in front of him.

At this, they both break into giggles.

"Something funny?" inquires the teacher.

"No sir," West states, confidently, accepting a piece of notebook paper from Maggie as well. The teacher's intrusion forces both of them to face forward and pretend to listen, as their instructor wastes no time in doling out their first assignment.

Scribbling down the essay parameters, Maggie sneaks a quick glance over at West.

Adel would have liked West. Maybe not his tattoos, but Maggie recalled how her mother was slow to judge anyone. Her mother's friends were diverse and unique—she didn't discriminate, since her work opened her up to all sorts of personalities.

Orion, on the other hand, would probably have had a heart attack, knowing that his little girl was pursuing a miscreant of this sort. Grounding her and stating that she wasn't allowed to date until college. Spouting the normal, generic, overprotective parental nonsense. Maggie often wondered if her behavior since their disappearance was a desperate cry for their return. That if she pushed the envelope, just enough, that maybe, just maybe, they would find her again.

She would give anything to be able to tell them both about this day.

And she realizes, for the first time since her parents, she is happy.

Chapter 10

E ve is miserable.

Smelling of burnt milk and ineptitude, her dress is ruined. Abandoning the bun entirely, her messy, dried, foam-filled hair sticks out in every direction. She needs a shower...and chocolate. Only a sugar high could temporarily distract her from the disaster that is her life.

Parked outside the high school, she finally spots Maggie heading down the steps, unusually chipper. At least one of them is having a good day.

Spotting Eve, she waves casually, unhurriedly strolling to the wagon. Maggie gets in, slams the door, takes one look at Eve, and snorts.

"Did you take a bath in coffee? Not that I'm complaining... you smell delicious!"

"Bertha hates me."

"Bertha...who is she? And why do I like her already?"

As Eve exits the parking lot, Maggie scans the students... until her shoulders slump. No luck. Her disappointment in not seeing West again is tangible. They apparently only have first period together, and she was hoping to catch a final glimpse. Yes, they will see each other again tomorrow, but the anticipation is already driving her mad.

Thankfully, Eve is a welcome distraction as she divulges to Maggie all that has transpired. Walking into the café feeling confident, and walking out feeling like she had been run over. Twice.

"If we weren't so broke, I would just tell you to quit. But I thank you for your sacrifice," Maggie teases, trying to cheer her up but doing a poor job of it.

"There is one thing that I didn't tell you...."

"And that is?"

"I met our new neighbors."

Maggie's palms slam onto the glovebox, thrilled.

"Me too! Well, I just met West! And what do you mean? All of them? Just two? Did they come into Jill's? What did they say?"

Maggie's questions are so numerous and rapid-fire that she only overwhelms Eve further. But her older sister tries her best to give her "the deets."

"The other four. You met the youngest? West? We'll come back to that. Okay, get this. Yes, they're brothers. There's Martin—he seems harmless, kind of nerdy. Rowan is way too into himself, the one with the braids? Total player. You. Avoid. That leaves...Tate, yuck, he's a brute. Serious anger issues if you ask me. And...Luca."

At his name, Eve pauses. For some reason, she doesn't want to talk about him.

For now, Luca will be off-limits.

"Brothers? I told you! Oh my God, where to do I start? I mean, how do I choose just one?"

Maggie looks as if she might explode in excitement. Normally Eve would be horrified, but she finds herself wistful. A little bit of Maggie's fire is back, and she doesn't want to put it out with her judgmental nature.

"Jill? What did Jill say?" Maggie inquires, enraptured.

"Jill, well...not much. At least not until they left. It was so weird! She turned frigid when she walked in from the back and they were standing there. I mean, she was downright hostile! All she told me later—and trust me, I tried—is that our families went way back. They're the Quinns, and apparently, we should stay away from them."

"Did you tell her that might be kind of hard, seeing as they are literally shacked up in the shack next to our shack?"

"I failed to mention that," Eve admits, pondering why she didn't divulge that pertinent detail to Jill.

"Lips are sealed, big sis!"

Maggie makes a zipping motion over her mouth and continues.

"Did you tell Jill that we're going to dig a hole and bury her stupid Dracula thing? That cutout creeps the hell out of me. Every time I go to the kitchen it's just *there*."

Eve chuckles, having forgotten about their cardboard guest.

"Yes! Apparently, she decorates the café every year for Halloween, and she wanted something that we wouldn't miss seeing, with the sticky note. Agreed, though, she could have made a better choice...."

Eve falls silent, pondering her choices recently and wondering for the zillionth time if she could have made better ones. The girls arrive home and Maggie cooks dinner for once, picking up on Eve's pure exhaustion. Nothing fancy, just canned spaghetti sauce and noodles with some semi-frozen meatballs (their arctic freezer being the likely culprit).

On the plus side—they finally have internet installed, and the speeds are somewhat respectable. It's the one luxury they can afford, apart from a shared cellphone plan. Curling up on their drop cloth-covered couch, the girls prop Eve's outdated laptop on a chair in front of them and watch an episode of some British show at Maggie's request. The eldest Abbott feels significantly better after her shower and a half-cooked meal. She could have fallen asleep right there, on that under-stuffed sofa, lulled by foreign accents and the warmth of Maggie by her side.

But for some reason, she resists.

Instead, pulling the necklace tucked beneath her shirt out, she studies it once again. For some reason, this piece of jewelry— that possibly belonged to June—is giving her comfort. In a way, she relates the chain and the pendant to herself. A small, lost thing, hoping someday that someone will find her...and when they do, she hopes that she, like this necklace, will be treasured.

A low-battery warning invades the laptop screen, to Maggie's protests. Checking the computer's clock, Eve notes that it's past ten. In order to be up early again tomorrow, she calls it a night, heading to her room. Splitting off on the second-floor landing, Maggie asks to borrow her laptop and charger, and Eve acquiesces. If Maggie wants to be exhausted for school tomorrow, that's her choice. Eve has done enough parenting for one day.

Crawling into her new soft bed, no sooner does Eve's head hit the pillow than she is fast asleep.

And dreaming.

I'm going to drown.

The circular tank that entraps me is filling.
Pounding my hands against the thick, transparent surface,
the sound reverberates.
Blue lights in the floor.
Evenly spaced, like a grid, embedded in the concrete.
They too, are trapped. They too, will never leave this room.
I am crying.
Ink-colored tears, staining the watery surface.
Seeing my faint reflection in the glass, how I have changed.
My gray skin.
My gray eyes.
My gray soul.
Shackled.
I am shackled to the floor of my watery tomb.
They are to blame. I know they are watching.
I cannot see them, but I know they are there.
In the shadows.
Always waiting.
The water is now to my waist. Soon, it will be to my neck. It
flows quicker, and quicker.
It caresses my chin.
I am going to die.
Today, this day, is my last.
My bitter sobs fall only on my ears.
And then, there is light.

"Wake up! Wake up, Eve, goddammit!" a gritty male voice
screams in the darkness.

Her eyes fly open.

Chapter 11

A wake. Eve is awake and covered in a cold liquid. Touching her bed, it's drenched as well. But in what? Water?

Smoke fills her lungs, making it hard to breathe. Bright flashes illuminate Eve's room, strobe-like, granting her glimpses of the ensuing chaos.

"We need to leave, now!"

"Martin, on your right!"

Someone shoves one of the figures toward her open door.

"Go get Maggie, we can handle this!" a deep voice bellows.

Maggie? That's right, Maggie is asleep. In the attic.

She will be fine, of course, because none of this is real.

Eve stretches, and yawns, waiting for yet another one of her twisted illusions to be over. Reaching to her nightstand, she locates her glasses and languidly plops them onto her face.

Weird, she always has perfect vision in her dreams. No glasses necessary.

Burning flesh stings her nostrils. The metallic smell of blood.

Double weird.

None of her dreams so far have been this vivid.

There is something in front of her bed. Large and black, its head almost brushing the ceiling. Attacked…it is being attacked. And it is angry.

Eve thinks she knows the attackers. They move with military precision, outfitted in black clothing and gear, their muscled arms fully exposed.

Tattoos. Uniform barcoded lines, just like the ones the Quinns have, but they are glowing red, alive and burning in their skin. The red tattoos flash with every attack, fueling their weapons as they distract the monster before them.

Eve chortles.

When she wakes up, she's going to write all this down.

One brother—with braids, so it has to be Rowan—is holding a bow. But the arrows appear to be sharp bolts of lightning, burning holes in her comforter as they miss their intended target. Thankfully, the saturated silk smothers their embers.

Bummer. Eve frowns—she really liked her new comforter.

Spotting a thick neck and angry scowl, there is no mistaking Tate. He is holding two spinning metal disks with edges alight and sparking. The black creature screams as he charges, strikes, and retreats. Tate's weapons connect with what she thinks is the monstrosity's stomach.

Sending out tendrils of smoke as quick as a snake, she can only see the beast from behind. Human-like in shape, it is easily eight feet tall. Smooth, black, hairless. Muscles grossly defined.

Wrapping her arms around herself, her teeth start to chatter.

"Dream. This is just a dream. I am dreaming…." Eve starts to mumble, so low that it barely registers in all the mayhem.

But the dark creature hears her.

And it stops, slowly twisting toward her.

Flash. She sees its human-like face and her mouth drops open in shock.

Bald. Ears. Nose. Mouth. Eyes. Everything is solid, terrifyingly black.

The monster's arms raise.

Footsteps. Someone runs across her old wooden floors, throwing their body over hers as the monster's tendrils spiral toward her head. But it's too late—the smoke grazes her cheek, burning into her skin.

She screams.

This isn't a dream.

This is really happening.

Another flash, a panicked face hovers above her.

"Luca?"

Chapter 12

Luca swiftly picks her up, holding Eve against his chest. He gives the monster a wide berth, while Rowan and Tate provide distraction with their arrows and saws. *Flash*. Eve spots Martin biding his time behind them. He pushes his glasses up on the bridge of his nose, a move Eve is all too familiar with, and she sees that Martin is holding two pulsing orbs. His hands squeeze, tattoos brighten, and the orbs start pulsing faster, and faster.

"I have her, let's move!" Luca orders, not waiting for their response. Still holding Eve to his chest as he runs toward the threshold, she peeks over his shoulder. Tate and Rowan are not far behind, but she watches as Martin kneels down, rolls the orbs toward the howling beast, and sprints to join their retreat. The orbs don't move in a straight line, but curve and randomly turn, frustrating and distracting the creature until they stop at its feet.

Eve misses the rest as they hurry down the stairs. From within her room, there is a *boom* and another bright flash. An unearthly, piercing howl, and darkness once more.

Arriving at the landing, there's a guy standing there who Eve assumes to be West. She fills with relief, spotting Maggie behind him.

Squinting in the darkness at West's glowing tattoos, Eve also notices that Maggie is holding an ax.

"Martin, how much time?" Luca rasps, quickly setting Eve down.

"Twenty seconds. Thirty if we're lucky."

A strong grip roughly turns Eve to face him. Luca. He bends over, his intense eyes inches from hers.

"Do you think you can run?" he questions, urgently.

Eve nods.

"Good. Go."

Eve doesn't move.

"Go!" he yells.

And this time, she does.

Grabbing Maggie's hand, they rush out the front door, across the porch, and down the driveway. Eve hardly notices the sharp rocks cutting her feet. She doesn't know where they are supposed to go—it's so dark, even the moon has been frightened into hiding.

West and Martin swiftly pass them, their odd tattoos thankfully illuminating the way as they turn, heading toward the Quinn home and the empty clear-cut field.

"Faster!" a male voice exclaims from behind. Rowan? Eve doesn't dare turn to look.

And then she hears it.

First inside the house and then out the front door, gaining ground, the boogeyman from within is out.

And it's coming.

Even with the adrenaline, Eve's legs start to tire, her lungs beg for her to stop, but they are almost there. For whatever reason, she knows they need to make it to that field. To the tall poles with the mounted panels and bulbs, which she now knows most definitely have a purpose.

Fifty feet.

Twenty-five.

Less than ten away, Eve's ankle connects with a rock and she trips, crashing to the ground.

"Eve!" screams Maggie, terrified.

Rolling onto her back, the eldest Abbott sits up and freezes.

Her eyes adjust. In the darkness, she makes out the creature from her bedroom.

And it is right in front of her.

"Close your eyes!" Luca yells from somewhere behind her. This time, Eve listens. Shutting them firmly, the entire world beyond her lids goes bright.

First, there is howling. Then the creature's blood-curdling shrieks—the noise is like nails scratching the inside of her skull. She covers her ears, eyes squeezed shut, and prays for all of it to stop.

Silence.

The world goes dark again.

Too afraid to look or remove her hands, she remains curled in a ball, shaking.

A callused palm squeezes her shoulder.

She jumps.

"Shh, it's okay. It's gone," Luca whispers.

Slowly opening her eyes, the huge light panels in the field emit a soft glow. Martin, holding a tablet, seems to be in control of their operation. A rotten stench, like overcooked meat, is wafting from the pile of ash in front of her. Panicking, she crawls backwards, desperately needing to put some distance between herself and…whatever that was. Only then does she get up and finally get a good look at their group.

Everyone is dirty. Small cuts with dried blood. But they seem to be mostly intact. Maggie's ax rests in the dried grass at her feet. She has her arms around West, who is holding her protectively. Maggie's racking sobs are buried in his chest. Her little sister has never been a crier; even when their parents' fate had been revealed, she had only pulled further into herself.

Eve's heart breaks, seeing her strong sister crumble.

Burning.

Her cheek is burning.

It feels like acid is eating into her flesh as she reaches for her cheek, but Rowan grabs her wrist, stopping her.

"Martin, get the pack!" he orders. Taking the bottom of his shirt, he rips off a strip, moving swiftly in front of Eve. Luca steps to the side, clearing the way, as Martin locates a black case in a duffel bag next to one of the lights, and heads back toward her.

The burning increases. Eve's fingers shoot toward her cheek, but are stopped again by firm, callused hands.

"Don't move," Luca warns, holding her wrists as Martin pulls out a vial.

She watches as Martin dumps the contents onto the black cotton strip from Rowan's t-shirt, now firmly wrapped around his fingers. Eve instinctively tries to pull pack as Rowan brings it toward her face, connecting with the wound.

Pain. Anguish beyond anything Eve has experienced. She struggles to break free as Rowan firmly holds his wet rag to the infected area.

Then it stops. Tears of torment turn into tears of blissful relief.

Relaxing, she shuts her eyes once more only to feel a firm tug on her neck. The sounds of a chain snapping and a loud hiss.

Eyes flying open, Eve sees her grandmother's necklace tossed in front of her tattered feet.

Boots. More running. A cloud of dust. Before Eve knows it, she is surrounded.

The Quinns form a circle, weapons raised, with Eve in the center.

"What the heck?" she squeals.

Looking into their hate-filled faces, she halts. When Luca speaks this time, it is low. Menacing.

"The necklace. Who are you working for?"

His boot comes smashing down on the pendant, crushing it into a thousand little pieces.

Chapter 13

"Eve, I am only going to ask you one more time. Who sent you?" growls Luca.

Pulling out a large, serrated blade from a holder at his side, he flips it, catching it again with ease. The moment the handle connects with his palm, the knife and his tattoos come alive once more. One by one, the brothers follow suit, until the eldest Abbott is surrounded by a glowing ring of muscle and malice.

"What are you doing! Eve? What is going on?" Maggie yells, trying to get to her sister. West swiftly puts a hand around her waist, pulling her out from the defensive circle. Tate and Rowan step closer to each other, closing the gap once more.

Something isn't right. Eve tries to focus on Luca—she knows that something important is happening. Looking to Rowan, Tate, Martin, and Luca again, she doesn't understand why their shiny weapons are pointed at her. Every thought feels like it's being pulled through maple syrup. Sticky, slow, and sweetly addicting.

Whatever is happening to her, she likes it.

Luca is speaking again, but her current state makes it impossible for her to concentrate.

She can't stop staring at his mouth.

Licking her lips, she starts to crawl toward his feet. Mid-slither, Eve realizes that the dry grass under hands feels amazing. The tingling sensation when it tickles her skin is pure ecstasy. Moaning, Eve flops over onto her back, running her arms and legs through the neglected lawn.

"What…is she doing?" Maggie whispers to West, horrified. She watches as Eve rolls back over and grabs a stick. With her new wooden friend, she starts to frantically dig.

Snap.

A loud crack of a whip to their right causes Maggie to wince. She quickly looks over her shoulder, as does everyone else, and Maggie is once again stunned into silence. Staring at the figure planted firmly in the driveway, she sees a tall woman. Toned, with red hair pulled back in a single tight braid. Raising her right arm, she cracks the whip once more, which upon closer inspection looks to be covered in razor-sharp blades. It sparks as it slices through the air.

Head to toe in black. A tight tank top exposing her arms. Her luminous red tattoos are identical in shape and size to the markings adorning the Quinns.

The creature before them is Eve and Maggie's aunt.

And Aunt Jill is pissed.

"Hi boys. How about you move away from my nieces, before I have to cut a few names from your family tree?"

Maggie is dumbfounded. Their aunt had always seemed like some crazy baking hippie. But the woman before them is a crimson-haired angel of death. The brothers shift, lowering their weapons. Even at five against one, healthy odds, Maggie could tell that none of them honestly wanted to challenge her.

"Your niece was wearing a lure! A goddamn lure! How do we know you didn't give it to her?" accuses Tate, pointing his blades toward her head.

Jill is stunned. She looks to Eve, silently begging for it not to be true.

"What is a lure—" begins Maggie, but West puts a finger to his lips, silencing her mid-sentence.

"I thought they were all destroyed," their aunt puzzles.

"They were. Only Snappers have them now."

The accusation in Luca's tone causes Jill to hiss in disgust.

"You think I gave it to her? Have my sacrifices not been enough to prove to you where my loyalties lie?"

"We have all made sacrifices," Luca grates, the words bitter in his mouth.

Maggie, beyond confused, is about to chime in again when something in Martin's backpack starts to beep. Everyone freezes—except Eve, who is now gnawing on what Maggie thinks in the semi-darkness is a pinecone.

Martin doesn't hesitate. Breaking into a quick sprint, he grabs the tablet he had used for the exterior light show minutes before and examines the screen.

"We've got four. From the north. Less than a mile away and closing fast. At their current rate of travel, three minutes."

And with that, everyone, including Jill, springs into action.

"I can't fit my nieces on my bike...." their aunt ponders, showing fear for the first time since her arrival.

"We'll take care of them," Luca promises, and Jill and Luca seem to come to some wordless truce.

"There is a safe zone! Meet me at the café!" she yells over her shoulder. Dashing into the woods and reemerging on a motorcycle, Jill speeds off purposefully down the dirt road, leaving her nieces' current protection in the hands of the Quinns.

Maggie's head hurts.

Hadn't Jill—just moments before—been challenging these guys? She was acting like Maggie and Eve needed to be protected from the Quinns. And now, they're all getting along because of Martin and his beeping iPad-like device?

But there is no time for questions. Grabbing her arm, West yanks her forward until they are both running toward the Quinns' porch and the sleek black hot rod parked out front. Maggie spots a floppy Eve in Luca's arms as Tate splits off, heading toward the moving truck. Within seconds, the tailgate starts to lower. But before it has even hit the ground, someone—Maggie thinks it's Rowan—disappears inside the truck. Then there's the unmistakable sound of an engine revving, tires against metal, and a giant black Humvee emerges.

Heading to the passenger side, Tate jumps in. Dust flies as the outfitted, monster of a vehicle barrels straight toward them.

Maggie had been wondering why they still had the moving truck parked in front of their house.

At least one of her questions has been answered.

The classic muscle car rips up next to the Humvee, and between the two, the headlights are blinding. Shielding her face, Maggie watches as Luca jumps out, barking orders, having already buckled Eve securely within.

"Maggie, Martin, with me! West, you're with Tate and Rowan."

Giving her hand a reassuring squeeze, West releases. They all split off to their respective vehicles, and no sooner are the doors shut than four massive orbs roll into view and stop.

Waiting.

Eve pushes her face against the glass; never has she seen anything so beautiful.

Perfect unearthly circles of ash and thunder. They look to Eve like crystal spheres belonging to a fortune teller, except for the fact that they are easily twenty feet tall. And unfortunately, more than likely there to kill them.

"Plan?" Luca asks Martin. Tablet in hand, he is in the front passenger seat with the Abbott sisters in back.

"Maggie, your hair? It's dancing...."

Eve, covered in dirt and debris, gazes at her sister in wonder through her filthy spectacles. She reaches to pull on a particularly bouncy ringlet, but Maggie slaps her hand away.

"Can you tell me now what's wrong with her?" Maggie inquires, whining as she continues to deflect her older sister's strange behavior.

"Forty-five degrees to the left, two hundred feet, then cut right back to the road. It would be advisable to avoid direct contact. All four are rollers—"

Luca growls, slapping his right hand against the steering wheel in frustration.

"I know that already! Rowan?"

Static, and then a voice comes through a square intercom on the dash.

"Copy that."

Eve pauses and gasps, thinking that a voice from heaven has just spoken to them.

"Jesus? Copy what? Copy what, Jesus?" she exclaims, hopeful, as she leans over Luca's headrest.

"Control her!" he bellows, pushing Eve back as he hits the gas. The Humvee does the same, following the hot rod's lead.

The rollers are right in front of them and coming just as fast.

They are going to hit the cars head on.

Both vehicles swerve left at the last second, shooting straight into the corn field. Eve giggles, clapping her hands in excitement, as Maggie's white knuckles cling to the headrest before her. Daring to look out the back window, at first, there is nothing. Just taillights and stalks of corn falling in the wake of the Humvee's carnage.

It a matter of moments, the rollers are back. Single file, consuming everything they touch, and gaining on them.

"Can't you just do that light thing and blast them? Like you did in the field?" begs the frazzled redhead, hoping the solution will be that simple.

"They are mutation level fours. That little trick won't work. Rollers' cells are repairing too quickly for such a small charge to be effective in disabling their molecular binding," Martin answers, not that Maggie understands a word of what he just said.

Eyes glued to his screen, pointer finger raised, Martin seems to be waiting. A nod, he points to the right.

"Now would be an optimal."

"Rowan!" Luca yells, cranking the steering wheel right, causing Maggie to slide left, crushing Eve against the door. The Humvee and the hot rod fishtail at first, but both drivers expertly straighten, changing direction in the field. Within seconds they hit the dirt road, and veer left. Maggie can't help but scream as the car tilts up, threatening to flip, but the tires lower and slam back into solid ground.

"Luca? Luca? Luca?" Eve pesters, relentless.

"What?" he snaps, irritated.

"Can you keep a secret?"

Silence. No response.

"I don't like you. But I like you. But I don't. But I do...." Eve's words trail off into a toneless melody.

"Can we tranquilize her?" Maggie snaps.

Both cars crank right, peeling onto Saints Street. Maggie looks over her shoulder again, and what she sees makes her heart stop. The black, spinning, circular orbs are inching closer by the second.

"Um, guys...?" Maggie voice cracks.

"We know," Luca and Martin state in unison.

The sun is starting to rise.

It has to be close to five in the morning as their high-speed chase delivers them into town.

Jill is already there, and she's been busy. Setting a trap of her own.

Large, plain, metal cylinders rise from strategically placed holes in the ground. Every twenty feet, another pole.

Their placement creates a rectangular perimeter around the main city buildings. Maggie spots Jill off to one side of the road with her motorcycle, illuminated by their headlights, before they roar past her. The moment the cars clear the rising metal rods, their brakes squeal as both automobiles fishtail before coming to a stop.

Whipping around, Maggie is just in time to see Jill tap the screen on a tablet she is holding before the poles erupt into a crisscross of lightning, creating a solid, electrified fence.

The rollers instantly try to reverse, but the one in front isn't so lucky; sliding into the fencing and Jill's snare, it howls. The noise of its torment rips at their ear drums as it explodes into blue light, smoke, and ash.

And then there are three.

Three rollers, waiting just outside the high-tech barrier.

Their vaporous surfaces roil and seethe.
The Quinns and the Abbotts are safe.
For now.

Chapter 14

Eve's eyes roll back into her head and she starts to convulse, her body held in place by her seat belt. Instantly, Maggie's attention is drawn from the ominous rollers.

"Eve? Eve? Oh my god, what's happening!" she cries out, but Maggie's door opens, and strong arms once again pull her away from her sister. Before she knows it, Rowan is holding her away from the vehicle while Tate and Luca gently retrieve Eve, laying her on her side against the frigid asphalt.

"Eve! Eve? Fucking let me go!" screams Maggie, her voice anguished, but Rowan doesn't budge.

Jill is next to her sister. Their aunt kneels down, checks her pupils and rises quickly.

"She isn't breathing. Follow me. Careful."

Luca, again, scoops up her now-limp sister and hurries after Jill. The rest of the Quinns follow. Arriving at the front of her café, they purposely head down the alleyway to the back, arriving at the red door. Maggie can see the perimeter fence sizzling as Jill flings the door open, holding it wide while they all rush in.

"Martin, the kit's in my office. The safe is under the rug at my desk."

Without question, Martin sprints through the kitchen.

"Luca, set her on the table. Tate, Rowan, West, get her ready."

Luca tenderly sets Eve upon the large metal surface, laying her on her back. Tate grabs her left wrist, pinning it down, as West does the same with her right. Rowan firmly grasps her feet as Martin re-enters with what looks like a pink shaving bag. Handing it to Jill, she unzips it, locates a large capped syringe with bright green contents, and sets it on the table. Jill snatches a pair of scissors hanging on the wall, then rushes back to Eve. Deftly, she cuts open her filthy t-shirt, stopping just before her breasts are exposed, and folds the fabric to each side.

Picking up the needle, she hands it to Martin, who leans over and locates an area between two ribs above her heart. Before Maggie can scream, he stabs it straight into Eve's chest. Emptying the contents, he removes the needle and backs away.

Silence.

No one speaks.

Maggie's horrified tears run slowly down the slope of her face, collecting at her collarbones.

And then Eve's chest starts to rise and fall. Rise and fall. She is breathing once more.

Maggie's knees buckle, feeling faint herself. Rowan catches her before she collapses, but she pushes him away, coming to lean against the table supporting her freshly revived sibling.

"Thank you for saving her life. Truly. I am so grateful…."

She takes a deep breath, then demands, "But what in the hell just happened?"

Silence. Brother looks to brother before Jill sighs, surrendering.

"Where do you want us to start?"

Chapter 15

Baking. Someone is making cookies. The smell of butter and chocolate chips wakens Eve. Disoriented at first, she looks at the ceiling, then spots the time cards on the wall...she's in Jill's office. Pushing off the couch, she slowly sits up as a soft, crocheted blanket slides to the floor. Shooting pains rip at her chest, causing her to fold forward. Gasping for air, she tries once again to straighten, pulling the oversized black t-shirt she's now wearing outwards at the collar. A dark purple bruise had formed in the center of her chest, and Eve is even more perplexed. The last thing she remembers is the field. They had made it to the field, and then everything after that was fuzzy.

What about Maggie? Is she alright? Forgetting her bruise, Eve has to find her.

Using the armrest to stand, gray sweatpants hang loosely around her waist. Forcing her left foot to move, then her right, she slowly walks to the door frame. Exhaustion pulls at her, tempting Eve just to sit. Sleep. But she has to find Maggie first.

As she gets closer to the exit, she thinks she hears lowered voices.

"Hello?" Eve's voice is raspy as she calls out.

Footsteps, then a small, beautiful ginger comes barreling from the kitchen. Eve breathes a sigh of relief as she is wrapped in a tight hug. Flinching from her injuries, Maggie releases her sister, worry written on her features.

"Shit, sorry! How are you feeling?"

"Okay, I guess. What happened?"

Maggie's smile falls as Eve notices West and Jill behind her. Her little sister looks to them before turning back to Eve.

"You want a cookie?" Maggie stalls.

"I want answers."

"Okay, but I want to stuff my face, so you're gonna have to watch me eat while we talk."

West and Maggie slowly guide Eve into the kitchen, while Jill magically retrieves a soft armchair from somewhere. Plopping into the heavily padded chair, Eve sighs, noticing two trays of chocolate chip cookies cooling on metal racks in the center of the baking table. Grabbing at least four, Maggie positions herself on a stool in front of Eve as she greedily munches away.

West and Jill pull up stools beside her.

"Are your brothers...?" Eve's first question is directed at West.

"They're fine. Just showering and packing, they should be back soon."

"Good. Good...." Eve sighs again. At least everyone had made it through last night alive. "What happened? In the field? Why did I pass out?"

"Umm, you didn't pass out. You were tripping on mutant poison for a solid ten, twenty minutes? I wish I would have recorded it," Maggie mumbles and starts to cough, the carbs stuffed in her jaw stunting her speech and laughter. Eve turns her gaze to Jill, who is oddly silent. She notices, for the first time, the intricate markings on her aunt's arms. Looking quickly to West for reference, and then back again to Jill, she puts two and two together.

"Wait…." Eve begins.

"Yup, Jill is one of them!" Maggie offers between bites.

"But, I… Well, you didn't have those a few days ago!"

"Makeup." Jill's voice is flat.

Before Eve can get more answers, the red door opens and in walks Luca, followed by Tate and Rowan.

Eve's aching chest tightens.

The three brothers have showered and changed. Outfitted in another version of black, which Eve guesses is more or less their uniform, she is instantly self-conscious. Touching her dirty, matted hair, she longs for some shampoo and something other than the formless fabric she is currently sporting.

"Look who's awake. Rough night?" Rowan flirts, grabbing a cookie for himself.

"She just woke up. Nothing has been explained," Jill snarls, hostile.

"We need to go," Luca interjects, all business all the time.

Luca and Eve's eyes meet. The intensity of his gaze sends heat to Eve's cheeks, causing her to flush. But she doesn't look away, or back down.

"Go where?"

"We can explain in the car. Everyone ready?"

Maggie, helping Eve to her feet once more, escorts her out into the bright sunlight. Squinting, Eve clings to her as their party of eight makes their way to the front of Jill's Coffee Shop. The other businesses are open, as it is midday. Strangers drive past, rolling carts full of groceries and talking on their cellphones as they continue to live their blissfully ignorant lives.

An elderly woman in a pretty yellow dress, holding a paper bag with her purchases, crinkles her nose at the site of Eve, spotting the eldest Abbott as she passes. Eve is not surprised—she agrees with yellow dress lady's assessment of her current state.

What *is* surprising is Luca's car parked in front of the café, now covered in dirt and grime. Maybe he had taken it off-roading? Parked beside it, a large Humvee with a metal grill and roof rack. Upon closer inspection, sporting what looks to be corn husks stuck to the inner edge of the windshield. Eve is too tired to ask as she's guided to Luca's car and belted by Maggie into the front passenger seat. Then her sister and Martin hop into the back, joining her in Luca's cramped two-door.

Looking to her right, Tate, Rowan, and West are contained within the Humvee as it roars to life. The only person left is Jill, who walks to Eve's window and taps on the glass.

Rolling it down, she shields her face from the sun and looks up at her aunt.

In the short time they've been in Saintsville, Eve has grown fond of their quirky relative. She doesn't know what part yet she played in all of this, or why their parents and Jill had their falling out, but Eve just knows she can trust her.

"Aren't you coming?" Eve asks.

"Sorry Evie, I can't. My assignment is here. But you're in good hands." Jill hesitates, not quite believing this herself.

"Assignment?"

"They will explain. I love you girls. I will see you soon."

Jill's sentiments are cut short as Luca reverses, leaving Eve and Maggie's aunt waving at the curb. Rolling up her window, she watches from the side mirror as Jill gets smaller and smaller, disappearing entirely.

Hurt. Eve is so sick of hurting. She is sick of caring that she's hurting. She is sick of finding a sliver of happiness, or a human connection, only for it be taken away. She is sick, most of all, of not knowing. Suffering from the burden of so many questions... but maybe now, she will finally get some answers.

And she feels like Luca, of all people, might just be able to help her understand.

"Wait, I thought we were going back to our house first. What about our stuff?" Maggie whines, realizing the direction they are heading is out of Saintsville.

"You can buy whatever you need when we get where we are going," Luca states gruffly.

"Can I buy you a personality? Because that would be first on my list...."

Surprisingly, Martin lets out a low chuckle.

"Those roller suckers are long gone, correct?" Maggie continues. "Don't be a prick, turn around!"

"Maggie, please. Can all of you help me to understand? What happened last night? What was that in my room? Why were you mad about the stupid necklace I found? Who are all of you, and why are we involved in all of...this? And where the heck are we going?"

Luca raises a free hand to silence her. He pauses, gathering his thoughts.

"Maybe we should start with your parents," he states cautiously.

What little color is left in Eve's tired cheeks disappears.

"You...know what happened to our mom and dad?" the eldest Abbott whispers.

Glancing at Eve, Luca's expression is unreadable.

"I do."

Chapter 16

"Your parents are like us. Or were like us. We are part of the Electric Mutation Task Force, EMTF, eliminating compromised citizens from the general population. The military slang word for us is 'Zappers,'" Luca says.

"Do you 'zap' zits too? Because that would be amazing...."

"Maggie, shut up. I want to hear this," Eve scolds.

"Do you want me to continue?"

With that, Luca adjusts the rearview mirror, staring Maggie down. She huffs, crossing her arms, and looks out at the endless sea of trees as they drive.

"Adel and Orion headed up the research and development side. But they were trained combatants, just like us. And yes, the United States government funds our operations so we can keep all of this under wraps."

"My brain hurts," Eve mutters. "Okay...so our parents were just like you. But what do you do? I mean all of you, what do you protect the rest of us from?" She pauses, her thoughts running a mile a minute. "Wait...did one of those things kill our parents?"

Eve's voice squeaks on the last part. Her fists clench, wanting to know, but also fearing the truth. Finding answers could be a double-edged sword—any possible explanation was bound to cut deep.

"Those 'things' were once like you and me. The scientific term is *Hominum mutata*, or 'changed man.' Almost all of our cells can generate electricity—electrical charges cause our heart muscles to contract, to beat. But what happens when your cells are overloaded?" Martin chimes in, unable to resist.

"Like X-men, sis, except Wolverine isn't a hot hairy old guy, and there is no such thing as a good mutant," Maggie adds.

"So, the mutation in my bedroom...was once like you and me?" Eve asks, surprisingly fascinated.

Peeling her now-blue nail polish off piece by piece, Maggie teases, "She catches on!"

"Correct. Changed, but unchangeable. Once a Snapper turns, we haven't—in our extensive research—been able to find a solution. Many argue within our sect that Snappers are the next form of evolution," Martin explains grimly. "That nature is preparing us for a pending natural disaster that will once again cleanse the planet, where only the strongest will be able to survive. They are the alpha species. The perfect killers. No conscience, they feel nothing. They desire nothing. Their only motivation is to hunt, to feed, and to eliminate. These mutations must be destroyed."

"They are bad mamba jambas!" Maggie snorts, unable to stay serious for very long.

"But with science, we are just as bad...." Martin smirks.

"What? Was that almost a joke? Martin, I think I'm starting to like you," Maggie retorts.

As Martin and Maggie continue to bond in the back, Eve shuts out their voices, too overloaded with information. So much of her and Maggie's childhood is starting to make sense. The importance of her parents' work, their constant absence. They weren't just trying to hack the DNA of plants to improve modern medicine…. Their parents had been working toward saving the entire human race. Or unchanged human race. Were the mutants still considered human? Or another species entirely?

Feeling eyes upon her, she looks over as Luca quickly snaps his attention back to the road, giving Eve a chance to study him in return.

His blonde eyelashes are thick, long, and soft, at odds with the severity of the rest of his features. She can see a small, moon-shaped white scar by his right eye, and a shadow of blonde stubble encasing his angular jaw. Wearing a long, solid black shirt, he had pushed the sleeves up to his forearms. The vivid red tattoos that had been alive the night before are back to black and dormant on his wrists.

She feels herself reaching up to fix her bangs but stops mid-gesture. *Ridiculous*. Her mild attraction to him needs to end—now. She reminds herself that the entire Quinn clan are murdering sadists. Technically they're killing humans who are already beyond redemption—but murder is murder, right? Unless it's a "kill or be killed" situation. In that case, are they doing the world a service with their particular set of skills?

Eve is too exhausted to argue with herself. Either way, Luca has to be a hard pass. If she wanted drama in her life, she just had to spend time with Maggie.

"Why do we call the changed humans 'Snappers'? Well, their DNA has quite literally snapped, fractured, and changed, triggered by a traumatic electrical event. They were rare. Only one or two occurrences per year due to natural causes. Then came appliances, outlets, power cords. Before Thomas Edison, or the invention of automobiles, the only real documentation in history of electric mutations was via lightning...." Martin continues but is interrupted by Maggie.

"And guess what? Badass Benjamin Franklin was the very first Zapper! He came up the grand idea of the lightning rod, to lure the naughty mutants out. Give them a nice zing, overload their already overloaded system, and boom! Mutant dust! Ha. Failed to teach us that part in history class, right?" she informs her little sister, smugly, before adding, "You should tell her about the necklace! That part is good...."

Crunch. Maggie dives into a bag of chips. How she could be hungry right now remains a mystery.

"What do you know about the lure you had around your neck?" questions Luca, his mood turning dark at the change in topic.

"Only that it was old looking. Did it belong to June?"

Eve touches her chest where the pendant had come to rest, feeling oddly naked without it.

"A lure is just that. A lure. What it attracts are Snappers. When it's turned on, the pulse it emits is irresistible—but it also protects the wearer. We had most of them destroyed, as you can see how that kind of power could be tempting. It not only lures, but it also controls. The electromagnetic pulse it emits is like a drug, and each pulse is like taking a hit. It addicts the Snappers to the possessor, giving them unequivocal domination."

"Domination, huh? Sounds a-lure-ing..." Maggie interrupts, sounding out "alluring" and laughing at her own joke.

"Do you ever stop?" Eve asks grumpily, but then asks, "Question. If I had the lure, and it was on, why did the Snapper attack me?"

"It didn't, it attacked Luca, who it thought was attacking you. But Luca wasn't aware of your possession of the lure in that moment, and thought he was intervening."

Martin's explanation makes perfect sense. Eve remembers having some sort of connection, as terrified as she had been. When it had been eliminated in the field, before the poison had taken over, she had a moment of sadness for the creature. The lure had not only been messing with the Snapper, but her as well.

"Imagine if a foreign government got ahold of that kind of technology. To have ultimate say over superhuman creatures, with no sense of right or wrong, the inability to question orders...."

Luca is cut off by Maggie, changing the subject.

"Did you know that the Snappers feed on electricity? They are voltage vampires!" As fascinating, informative, and exhausting as this conversation has been so far, Eve's patience is wearing thin. Her further questions about Snappers and Zappers are sure to be extensive, but Luca and Martin hold the key to the one thing that has haunted Eve and Maggie for the past four years.

Eve takes a deep breath and re-asks the most burning question of all.

"Can you tell us what happened to our parents?"

Luca doesn't answer right away, hesitating. His eyebrows furrow. Looking over again, Eve is surprised to see a new emotion on Luca's ever-stern features.

Worry.

"Alive," he admits finally. "Very much alive."

Of all the things Luca could have said, Eve was not expecting this. Eyes wide as saucers, she whips to look at Maggie behind her.

Of course, Maggie already knows, adding bitterly, "And they faked their deaths, murdered a bunch of Zappers, and are currently wanted fugitives."

Maggie's words send chills down Eve's spine. "Not possible..." she utters, shaking her head in disbelief.

"Yes possible," Maggie continues, "Oh yeah, I'll explain later. They also sent the rollers, you missed that part. Apparently, Mom and Dad are now trying to kill us too...."

Turning back to look at her baby sister, Eve and Maggie communicate wordlessly, both thinking the same thing.

Why?

Chapter 17

After the rough explanation by Maggie about their mom and dad being evil villains, the entire car falls silent. Each person seems lost in their own story. Eve is struggling with the truth, finding it hard to believe that their parents would harm anyone intentionally. If anything, she just pulled further into her shell.

Don't murderers give clues as to their true nature? Adel and Orion hadn't been violent or cruel. They had been strict but loving. Bedtimes and curfews and the implantation of manners, most of which Maggie had undone the moment Eve was left in charge. But they had game nights, and frisbee tosses in the park, and Orion was always helping them with their homework.

Eve wonders what she and Maggie had done so wrong that their own flesh and blood would throw them away. How could they be rejected by their own parents?

Or was all of this some sort of giant misunderstanding?

Maggie seems resigned to the fact that Orion and Adel are alive and have sinister motives, but Eve can tell that she's also furious. A typical Maggie move, covering her rage with humor. The more that Maggie is in pain, the more sarcastic she becomes, hiding her true feelings behind her laser-quick wit.

Not that she can blame her younger sibling for her fury.

Their dear parents have been alive all this time and haven't reached out once. More than likely observing from afar. They have watched their daughters run out of money, sell most of their possessions, and hit a point of desperation, forcing them to leave the only home they had ever known.

But if they're hunting them, why now?

What had changed? As her eyes begin to droop, the questions never stop bombarding her consciousness.

Eve doesn't remember falling asleep. The throbbing of her chest wakes her up occasionally. Every time her eyelids part, the landscape has changed. From trees and forests to desert once more. From morning to night. Luca never seems to tire, a constant driving force carrying them away from Saintsville.

What are Eve and Maggie to do now?

The few possessions they had brought with them they would likely never see again.

Maybe Jill could forward Eve's books? Gather them up, stick on some postage, and pop them in the mail? But Eve has a feeling that wherever they are going, the postal service more than likely doesn't deliver.

Still in the same borrowed clothing, Eve hardly noticed that someone has loaned her a hoodie as well—one she doesn't remember putting on. The faint scent of aftershave leads her to believe that the owner is probably one of the guys located within the two cars.

As the vehicles climb, heading to a higher elevation, the terrain changes once again. Woodsy, like Saintsville but colder. She can feel the temperatures dropping and is grateful for the oversized warmth the sweater lends. The clock on the dash reads 4:30. Eve assumes a.m. because of the absence of sunlight and Martin and Maggie being fast asleep in the back. Maggie's soft, whistling snores are Luca and Eve's current soundtrack.

Luca has noticed that Eve is once again awake, but she takes to reading the mile markers for companionship.

"Are you thirsty?" Luca offers her an unopened water bottle, removing it from a convenience store bag. They must have stopped for gasoline and bathroom breaks, but she must have slept straight through.

Licking her lips, she notices they're dry and cracked. He's right to offer water, and she gladly accepts with a mumbled, "thanks." Turning the cap slowly until the seal breaks, she starts to take small sips, thinking their interaction is over.

"You should probably know that we followed you from Seattle. Most of us were assigned to your surveillance after…the attack at the lab, with Orion and Adel."

Eve starts choking, some of the water in her mouth accidentally entering her windpipe. Shifting at the noise, Martin adjusts his jacket he is using as a pillow but doesn't wake. Maggie is still out cold.

"Four years? Enough! Seriously, enough revelations!" Eve whispers through her coughs.

Luca taps his fingers against the steering wheel. Small talk is definitely not his strong suit. "I thought you would take comfort in knowing."

"What? How is that comforting? That you've been 'keeping an eye on us' for quite literally, years? I already have enough of my past to rethink, without having to sift through my memories and see if any of you somehow look familiar. That maybe I saw you, or Rowan, or Tate at the movies and didn't realize you weren't just there to watch a flick. That you were there as an insurance policy, because God forbid anything happened to us."

Eve keeps her voice low, but her words are venomous.

Luca shrugs. Unperturbed. "We had our orders."

"Orders? To keep us alive? Ha, such a waste. If you haven't noticed, we're nothing special…." Without warning, Eve is crying. All of it, everything, is just too much.

She quickly wipes away her tears, only spreading around the dirt, creating muddy lines on her smooth skin. Tucking her knees to her chest, she pulls up the hood and leans against the chilled window glass.

She has never been more confused in her life, and a lot of very confusing events have led up to this. Her emotions are a pinball machine. Angry, frustrated, afraid, heartbroken, hopeful, and overall, overwhelmed. Not that she particularly liked their new home, but at least it was a home. She would happily go back to the way things were less than forty-eight hours prior. Before all her preconceived notions of their family were totally, and utterly, destroyed.

Eve realizes that she had been partially listening to Maggie and Martin's continued discussion, having been awoken by their chatter at some point during the night. In her sleepy haze, she had learned some things.

Their parents were apparently traitors. They were caught by the EMTF experimenting on mutants, creating new variations, but managed to allude capture. Hence, the lab, the blood, and their disappearance. Not daring to contact their daughters for fear of being caught, they chose instead to become Zappers. Snappers are mutants, Zappers hunt Snappers, and Changers— they are the worst of all. To turn a person, basically hitting the off switch on their soul, and then modify them into horrifying abominations? Changers change people into the unchangeable.

Their parents are farmers, and what they harvest are mutants. Eve's heart aches, and not just because it's been stabbed by a thick needle.

Closing her eyes once more, she pretends to fall back asleep, but feels the wheels turn and the change from pavement to gravel as they exit the freeway. She can't help but open her eyes and look out. The shift in roadway seems to be a cue for Martin to stir and Maggie to yawn.

No longer obligated to interact solely with Luca, Eve's tears have dried, and she's relieved by her sister's gravelly, "Are we there yet?" as she stretches.

"We are roughly six-point-forty-three kilometers from our destination," Martin informs everyone, that tablet he's holding seeming to be a frequent extension of his arm.

"Whatever. As long as it gets me out of this car," states Maggie grumpily.

Eve couldn't agree more.

With the sun rising, she notices the dirt road they're on is heading straight toward a heavy iron gate. Tall, solid stone walls intersect the singular metal point of entry, extending for what looks like miles to the left and right.

Whatever this place is, it's heavily fortified, and—no surprise—in the middle of nowhere.

As they get closer, she thinks she can make out a cursive letter "E" on the thick, iron bars.

"Welcome to Evergreen." says Luca proudly. And for once, he's smiling.

Chapter 18

The gate is tall and imposing. At first appearance it's weathered, belonging to some grand estate. Eve figures that anyone out for a drive who happened to stumble upon this place would be curious, wondering what was contained within the walls. But they wouldn't give it a second thought, chalking it up to old money and a strong desire for privacy.

Looks can be deceiving, as the strategically placed cameras in the trees scan their cars before the intimidating gate swiftly opens. They pass through, and just as quickly, the gate slams shut—a thick, metal motorized bar sliding into place, reinforcing the entrance behind them.

Eve and Maggie can't help but stare out the small car windows in wonder.

"Well, I guess sneaking out isn't going to be an option," Maggie states matter-of-factly.

Tall pine trees line the long driveway, and before Eve knows it, they're pulling up in front of a massive mansion.

It is unlike anything she has ever seen before.

At first, she thinks it is a log cabin, but it looks more like they've stumbled upon a ski resort...minus the snow. Though if the cold is any indication, that weather condition is imminent.

The main house is stunning, with its large pitched roof and tall, arched windows. There are at least three levels, and the same stone from the walls surrounding the property has been worked into the structure. The contrast between the wood logs and stone columns is warm and inviting.

Even more spectacular—to the left of the main house, steam rises from hot springs that flow off a natural hill, pouring water into a pool below, essentially creating a small-scale waterfall.

The house is quiet, probably due to the early hour, as the Humvee and hot rod park in the circular driveway. Farther to the left is a large, square log building and a few smaller structures beyond that. Luca, still smiling, exits from the car the moment it is parked, and Eve takes that as her cue to do the same.

Car doors open and close as the five Quinns and two Abbotts gather in front of wooden steps, leading to a covered balcony and a large, solid timber threshold.

"Is skinny dipping allowed?" Maggie whispers to West suggestively, indicating the tempting pool mere feet away.

His shaggy blonde hair is tied black in a low ponytail, a few pieces having escaped. With the mist coming off the water and his bare glistening arms, he could be on the cover of a romance novel. Eve watches as West looks at Maggie, raises an eyebrow, and smirks.

Maggie's mischievous grin as a response would have normally set off warning bells in Eve's head—but West, of all the Quinns, is growing on her. He has been nothing but polite and thoughtful—unlike the usual riffraff Maggie brings home.

So wrapped up in the budding teen romance, Eve hardly notices Rowan, now standing beside her.

"Not a bad suggestion," he says. "If you haven't noticed, you're quite rank...."

Without thinking, Eve smacks his arm, stifling a smile herself. She is about to ramble something about how Rowan should invest in a comb when the front door is thrown open, and a chestnut blonde in a flowery bathrobe, flannel pajamas, and slippers bolts out.

She scans the group, takes one look at Luca, and squeals.

Running down the stairs, she throws her arms around him, burying her head in his neck.

Eve grinds her teeth.

This gorgeous woman, who could be anywhere from her late teens to early twenties, with her shiny long, wavy hair and a perfect figure, is now standing in front of Luca talking animatedly. Eve is instantly annoyed.

Jealous, though she would never admit it.

Glancing down at her soiled clothes, she has never felt more inadequate.

Rowan cups his hands around his mouth and yells, "Beth! Stop playing favorites!" and laughs. Catching the attention of the beautiful woman, she breaks away from Luca, squeezing his shoulders, and jogs over to Rowan, engulfing him in a giant hug as well. She does the same with Tate, and Martin, saving West for last. As he picks her up and plants a solid kiss on her cheek, Eve notices that Maggie seems both fascinated and irritated.

The pretty stranger is smiling from ear to ear when she finally seems to notice the Abbotts. Looking between each of them, she nudges West with her elbow—an indication that he should introduce her.

"This is Beth. Beth, Maggie, and the rough-looking one over there is Eve."

Beth playfully rolls her eyes at West's description of the eldest Abbott and strolls directly over. Before Eve can protest, she's receiving a hug as well.

"I am so sorry that you have had to spend so much time with my brothers!"

Brothers. Wait. Beth is their sister?

As if reading her mind, the newest Quinn responds.

"Yup, I'm the normal one. And now, let me take both of you inside. I'm sure you would like to see your room?"

"'Room'? Not 'rooms'? Nope. Not sharing," Maggie whispers. Eve gives her a "knock it off" look, which seems to work.

Confidently, Beth heads up the stairs, motioning for the Abbotts to follow. The rest of the Quinn clan hangs back, giving the girls some space to get acquainted.

Stepping through the front door is exactly like entering the lobby of a hotel, minus the check-in desk or restaurant with a bar. Leather couches and rustic chairs surround a large stone fireplace on the right, with the entire room opening up to a glass ceiling. Eve counts three levels, with staircases on either side.

Moving to stand in the middle, she can see that they're in the center of a half circle. Each level has an evenly spaced number of closed doors, partially hidden behind the intricately carved wood railing. All the doors need are numbers, and then they would've definitely been in a resort. Maybe Evergreen had been at one point? She would have to remember to ask Beth.

Here, at Evergreen, a calm has come over her.

Here, for some reason, Eve actually feels safe.

With her guard dropped, she realizes just how depleted she really is.

Linking Eve's arm in hers like they are old friends, Beth pulls her to the staircase on the right and keeps pulling her, all the way to the third floor. Coming to a door with a bear carved on the front, she turns the handle and opens. Stepping aside, Beth motions for Eve and Maggie to enter first.

The room is simple. Two identical canopy beds on opposite ends, with red checkered comforters and matching pillows. Adding to the splendor is a large oak dresser placed just below a small window. With the tan curtains pulled back, Eve can see the driveway and the clouded mountains beyond. The best part of the room is the middle doorway, because it connects to an even more charming bathroom.

Fluffy white towels are stacked on the stone-built sink, with a white porcelain basin. Eve wants to cry after spotting the large tub and walk-in tiled shower beside it.

"Can I be rude, and just tell both of you to get out?" Eve begs, turning to Beth and Maggie.

"But then I'm going to have to clean the shower, after you take a shower, before I take a shower. Who knows what you're harboring right now." Maggie mock cringes as Eve sits on the edge of the tub, kicking off her sneakers and slowly removing one sock at a time.

Beth grabs Maggie's hand, escorting her away. Eve hears Beth's melodious voice say, "Come on, there is an extra bathroom a few doors down…" and the rest is muffled as sweet Beth closes the bathroom door.

Eve is finally alone.

Chapter 19

She doesn't know how long her shower lasts, shampooing her hair over and over before the water finally runs clear. Getting out, Eve finds lotion in the cabinet, and it stings as it makes contact with the many partially healed cuts she has acquired. Taking a towel and wiping the steam from the mirror, she puts on her glasses, finally getting a good look at her face.

Eve had completely forgotten about the burn from the smoker, prominent on her cheekbone. *Smoker.* The Quinns' slang for the mutation level one that had lashed her with its poisonous vapor. Leaning in for a closer look, it appears like it should hurt, but it strangely doesn't. Thin and long, as if her face had been snapped by a guitar string, that particular wound is almost healed. Other cuts and bruises mar her usually perfect skin. Noticing her cracked lips, she hunts around the unopened toiletries basket that has been left, finding a tube of ChapStick.

A knock at the door causes her to startle, dropping the lip balm into the sink.

"Eve?" says Beth, just outside.

"Yes?"

"I brought you some clothes. I'll just leave them here."

Beth is growing on her too.

"Thank you so much," Eve says genuinely.

"Breakfast is ready as well, but if you just want to sleep, no one will bother you."

Footsteps fading away indicate that Beth has graciously exited once more.

Towel firmly wrapped, Eve turns the door handle and looks down to find a set of soft-looking navy pajamas, a lighter-blue fluffy bathrobe, and matching slippers that looked to be around her size.

She had never been more appreciative in her life.

Barely getting the shirt over her head and the pajamas pants pulled on, Eve doesn't even bother with the bathrobe and slippers as she exits to the main bedroom. Maggie, in a similar set but purple, is already lounging on one of the beds, drying her hair with a towel.

"You going to breakfast?" Maggie inquires.

"Nope."

And that is all that Eve mumbles before she climbs onto the mattress, pulls the covers up, and falls quickly and deeply asleep.

Maggie, having had a solid six hours of somewhat uncomfortable backseat car rest, is wide awake. Somewhere in the back of her mind, she knows that she should be doing the same as her extremely practical older sister, but she feels like a kid at a theme park. Too much to see, too many guys to experience.

Maybe girls, too—Beth is a cutie.

Exiting their shared room, Maggie looks over the railing and all the way down to the first floor, spotting random bodies milling about. Some she knows, a few she doesn't. Tate is talking to a middle-aged, muscular black man. They seem to be arguing, which is not surprising when Tate is involved. Her attention is drawn to two new faces. Both female, Hispanic, with similar features. Long, straight dark hair, tan skin, and big brown eyes. Both of them are extremely attractive, which seems to be a pre-requisite for associating with the Quinns.

Maggie leans on the railing, observing the Latinas as they hold their coffee mugs and chat with Luca. One of the two girls keeps touching his arm, which Maggie feels inclined to do something about. Yeah, sure, when the carload of brothers first poured out in Saintsville—what now felt like decades ago, not days—Maggie would have gladly hooked up with any or all of them. But she had seen the way Eve behaved whenever Luca was near. Nervous, aggressive, fidgety. Eve only gets that way when she's attracted to someone, and Maggie is secretly rooting for a possible romantic connection. She is team Eve, and about to block some unnecessary interference.

Making her way downstairs, she's the only person draped in fabric with any sort of color, the rest of the bodies in predictable black. To her eyes, their matching tattoos are getting old. It's like they're all in some fraternity, and if you don't have the lines, you don't belong.

"Good morning!" Maggie says loudly, sidling up to the trio. "I'm Maggie! Hi. I've been watching both of you throwing your-selves at my friend here from all the way up there, thought I'd come to rescue him...."

Maggie is just warming up.

"Ladies, sorry to disappoint, but the only thing Luca is attracted to is his car."

Both bronzed beauties pull back, flustered.

"You are…?" Maggie asks, then adds, "Hello, manners!" Extending her hand, she shakes each one of the girl's limp fingers.

"I am Sophia, this is my sister Lucia…." utters the seemingly older of the two.

Not easily deterred, Sophia places a manicured hand on Luca's chest, and smiles.

"I will see you later, yes? Lucia, let's go."

Maggie tries to study Luca, gauge his response, but he is always so nonreactive. Removing her claw, Sophia ignores Maggie entirely as they turn and saunter away.

Unsure of what to do next, after successfully solidifying two new enemies, Maggie's stomach grumbles loudly. A tap on her shoulder causes her to look, only to be pleasantly surprised.

West leans in, his words only for her ears.

"You should be careful with those two. They don't play fair."

Reaching up, he gently pulls on one of her spiral locks, and releases.

"How long have you wanted to do that for?" she teases.

"A while," West admits, and they both laugh. Playfully throwing his arm around her

shoulder, he guides her toward the front entrance and then to the right. They head down a short hallway, into the kitchen, greeted by the delicious aroma of sizzling bacon.

Of course, a house like this has a grand gourmet kitchen sporting multiple ovens. A plump, gray-haired woman in charge of grub is skillfully grating cheese, lifting lids on pots, and flipping pancakes at the exact right second. Distracted by the large breakfast buffet, Maggie grabs a clean plate from a stack and dives in.

West chuckles at the sight of the tiny girl with the huge plate of food. "Twenty bucks you can't eat all of that."

"I'm currently broke and homeless. Darn. So. New rules? I win, you give me twenty, you win, I make out with you."

At this, West actually blushes. It takes a moment before he responds, grabbing two more biscuits and stacking them onto her plate.

"Well, I'm just going to have to make sure I win."

Grabbing a strip of bacon and taking a bite, Maggie tries to hide the butterflies in her stomach. She can easily finish the contents of her large plate—the pile of food isn't just for show.

But this is one bet she wouldn't mind losing.

Chapter 20

I didn't drown.

I remember my screams as the cold liquid finally pulled over my head.

I remember my lungs filling.

And I remember the sudden anger. Rage.

The water started to boil and seethe around me, swirling faster and faster.

I should have been frightened.

Trapped, unable to breathe, but in that moment I once again changed.

Crack. The translucent barrier surrounding me started to fracture.

I stopped struggling. I stopped fighting. I let the darkness in.

And when I did, the entire tank exploded outward.

The water rushed away from me, breathing a sigh of relief as it hugged the cement.

I coughed and heaved, but my rage did not lessen.

My hands throbbed as I looked down at my wrists, still chained to the floor.

Turning my left palm to face upwards, a piece of the glass protruded from it, slick with blood.

Footsteps.

Grinding, as the heavy paneled metal door to the room was pulled open.

Someone entered.

The blue lights in the floor faintly illuminated the older woman before me.

White lab coat. Dark brown hair pulled back into a tight bun. Crystal blue eyes, piercing me with their hatred. I know her.

Mom?

And then everything went black.

I didn't drown, but a part of me died in that tank.

Rocking back and forth, I now cradle my bandaged hands against my chest.

I am awake.

Once again, in the white room.

Eve bolts straight up in bed, disoriented. Her breath comes rapidly as she searches frantically for her mother. Sweat beads on her forehead and her heart pounds. Scanning the space, it takes a moment before she realizes where she is. Evergreen. The room with the bear on the door. The Quinns. Beth. It all comes flooding back. Her mother, Adel, is nowhere to be found.

She can still smell the chlorine of the water in the holding tank, and a phantom ache from the restraints on her wrists. The white room. How cold it was, how small. She feels tainted, twisted, and utterly wrong. These visions seem to be poisoning her, slowly destroying the already-thin line she walks between sanity and total destruction.

Maybe her conversation with Luca and Martin on the car ride here triggered this particular episode? All the talk about their parents has been damaging. At least that's the case for Eve. Adel and Orion had always been idolized—her smart, strong, capable mother and father that sacrificed so much in the pursuit of science. But what do you do when the two people that you love most in the world turn out to be nothing but an illusion? They are all smoke and mirrors.

Warm light flows through the open curtains as Eve starts to calm.

On impulse, she raises her left hand, turning it from side to side. Pausing, Eve notices for the first time a faint white line on her palm.

A scar. The same hand, and in the same place where the glass had been in her dream. She shudders, and then—

Boom.

The door flies open and her head whips toward the noise. Sure enough, a red-headed blur races over to Eve's bed, and leaps, landing at her feet.

"Yay! You're awake! Good!" Maggie exclaims. "You have to see this!"

Clapping her hands together, Maggie scoots and jumps to the floor, heading swiftly to the exit. Eve can hear her feet running down the stairs, not waiting for Eve to join her.

Groaning, the eldest Abbott throws herself back into the pillows. Suddenly, she wants to stay in this room forever. Any encounter with the Quinns only seems to lead to total embarrassment. And, wild guess, whatever Maggie wants to show her more than likely involves them. Her stomach disagrees as it growls loudly. Not quite sure how many meals she has missed, her appetite has come back with a vengeance.

Giving in, she hurries to the bathroom and is happy to find another stack of clothing waiting. She tries on a sports bra, fitted shirt, and loose linen pants, all of which fit, finishing her look with black combat boots. Evergreen must have a supply closet, or Eve and Beth are the same size.

Splashing cool water on her face and retrieving her now-cracked glasses from the tile counter, she is pleased to see that her bruises have faded to a brownish green. The small cuts are healing nicely, and the burn from the Snapper is even less prominent. Throwing her hair back in a ponytail, she fluffs her bangs and sighs.

Maybe at some point in her life she would stop being a hot mess.

Maggie didn't really leave her with any specific instructions of where they should meet. Heading from the third floor down, she doesn't see a single soul exiting any one of the many rooms, but low voices faintly echo from somewhere within the home. The sound of talking and laughing increases, and so does the smell of delicious food, as Eve follows her ears and nose to the kitchen.

Stepping through the hallway into the open space, her eyes widen in astonishment. She is standing in another large room. Floor-to-ceiling glass windows look out to an open field of tall grass, bending and straightening in the wind. So entranced by the view, she startles when a voice asks her, "Hungry, dear?"

A plump woman with gray hair, her face full of friendly creases and folds, offers her a plate full of food. Eggs, bacon, breakfast potatoes, and toast. Before Eve can thank her or catch her name, the cook has already turned, heading back to retrieve something from the oven. Looking at her meal, Eve is strongly tempted to sit straight down onto the floor and rap-idly shove every morsel into her hungry mouth. That is, until she glances over to the right and notices the large dining table and its occupants.

Planted in a middle chair, Martin is munching neatly on a few slices of dry toast and reading what seems to be a newspa-per. The brainy Quinn isn't so bad—he would more than likely ignore her presence, not that Eve feels like doing anything but eating. On the other hand, Tate, at the head of the formidable oak slab, scowls in her direction. Stabbing a syrup-soaked waf-fle, he shoves it into his grinding jowls. His aggressive chewing could not be any clearer that she is not welcome. To the left of Tate are two women she doesn't recognize. Their shiny, ink-black hair plated into identical French braids. Eyeing Eve, the strangers seem to be evaluating her. She studies them as well, noticing that their clothing is identical to what had been left for her to wear.

Pulling her shoulders back, she realizes that she is being ridic-ulous. This isn't middle school—they aren't the popular girls, and she doesn't need their permission to sit at their table. Her appetite at the moment is greater than her need for approval.

She makes a decision and steps toward them, only to freeze at the sound of two male voices echoing down the hall she had just traversed through. Recognizing one of the two, she suddenly has goosebumps.

It has to be Luca…but Luca and someone else are in a heated exchange. Eve quickly walks over to the table, choosing a place setting next to Martin, and drops her plate down with a clank. Pulling out her chair, she hurls herself into the seat and begins to eat, not daring to look up.

"No. No. Riley, my answer is final. Babysitting those brats was bad enough, but not this," Luca utters heatedly.

"There is no one else, Luca. Most of your brethren are stationed at their posts. With our dwindling numbers, you and your brothers are the only option," demands another deep voice, one she doesn't recognize.

"Then see who wants to volunteer! I will take up their post, they can come here. What you are asking me to do is impossible," Luca practically begs.

"Enough. This is final. If they agree, I am signing off. Am I making myself clear?"

Then both voices fall silent, noticing the back of the hunched girl silently eating her food. Two pairs of boots start to move in Eve's direction, and her muscles stiffen. Regretfully, she lowers her fork, and goes to push her chair back when a strong hand stops her. Slowly looking up, she takes in the powerful form of the man beside her.

Easily six-foot-four and musclebound, his smooth black skin is etched in the same tattoos as the Quinns, but more extensive. Faint black lines climb past his shirt, and all the way up his neck, covering half of his face. Eve has never seen someone more intimidating in her life—that is, until his scarred features break out into a wide, gap-toothed grin.

"You must be Eve. I have already met the infamous Maggie. I'm Riley, and this is my home."

Extending his sizeable hand, Eve gives it a firm shake and finds herself smiling in return. Riley, like Beth, has an easygoing charm. Thinking of the Quinn sister, she realizes she has yet to see her this morning...or Maggie, who asked her to come down in the first place. As if reading her mind, Riley pulls out Eve's chair, giving her no choice but to hurriedly stand.

"Time for eating later. We don't have a second to waste."

Riley turns, marching to another doorway to the right of the room which Eve hadn't yet noticed. On the solid, log-stacked wall hangs a framed oil painting. Romanesque in style, it depicts scenes of war. Horses, spears, swords, and death. Desperate souls fighting for their fragile mortality. Firmly planted in the middle of the wall—surrounded by the painting—is a circular, windowless tunnel. Dimly lit, it dips, hiding where it may lead. Eve glances at Luca. His fists are clenched, as he glares icily at Riley, frozen next to the long kitchen counter.

He had mentioned "babysitting those brats." It could only be her and her sister that he was referring to. With that realization, Eve feels her heart harden—her attraction toward him lessening.

Luca may be physically impressive, but his total lack of respect is repulsive.

"Eve, with me please? You too, Luca."

Riley is standing in the archway to the tunnel, waiting. Next to him are the two attractive strangers. They had to be sisters, even down to the fake identical smiles they flashed Eve's way.

Choosing Riley and the Latinas over one more second near Luca, Eve hurries to join them.

"Where are we going?"

Riley's chuckle reverberates, bouncing off the solid walls as they walk. "You'll see...."

Groaning internally, all Eve needs is one more surprise.

Chapter 21

As they move deeper underground, Eve's anticipation grows. The longer they walk, the greater her curiosity. Ultraviolet light shines around Riley's large frame, throwing him into silhouette as they finally come to what the tunnel is connected to.

Which is nothing like Eve has ever encountered.

Her first thought is of laser tag on her seventh birthday. The cheaply constructed rooms covered in invisible ink, alive under the black lights. But she isn't seven and this isn't her party.

This is a training ground.

They're standing at the entrance to a large, subterranean gymnasium. Voices yell, and bodies are thrown to the ground as individuals spar. Their barcoded tattoos are crimson and shining. The main commotion seems to be emanating from the center, where a small group has gathered, hooting and hollering over two combatants circling each other.

Eve's jaw drops when she spots Beth as one of the two. Her opponent, Rowan. The gentle blonde from last night has vanished. Her hair—pulled back into tightly woven braids kissing her scalp—changes her appearance entirely. No longer soft and gentle, this woman is ferocious. She hadn't noticed Beth's tattoos before either, her clothing having concealed her true nature.

Feinting a punch to the left, Beth slaps Rowan smack in the face with her right hand. Tasting blood, Rowan ignores his split lip and continues to circle.

Everything next happens so fast. Rowan charges and spins into a roundhouse, but Beth ducks and rolls, coming up behind him. She kicks his back, sending him face-first to the mat. He rolls as well, coming to his feet, and they are once again facing each other.

Eve and Maggie had both been forced to take martial arts, right up until their parents' disappearance. Mostly tae kwon do, with a bit of *kyokushin* and *krav maga*. Fridays had been Eve's least favorite, since she never understood why her brainiac caregivers were so fixated on their daughters knowing self-defense. Many years have passed since Eve has been in a studio, but she remembers enough to know that this is no ordinary sparing match.

This makes Eve and Maggie's years of forced instruction look like child's play.

Rowan charges his sister once more, but before he knows it, Beth has grabbed his arm and thrown her weight into his middle, flipping him over her body. Holding his right arm at a painful angle, Beth has him pinned, and for a moment he resists before tapping out.

The bystanders roar and whistle, while Beth helps her older brother to his feet. No hard feelings between the two as Rowan bows to her, before grabbing her head in a headlock and gently ruffing up her braids.

"I didn't know Beth was a Zapper," Eve says, more to herself, in awe of what she has just witnessed.

"Beth is the deadliest of all of us," Martin states, appearing beside Eve. His calm, almost bored demeanor leads Eve to believe that this is an everyday occurrence.

The lines on Rowan's and Beth's arms dim back to black, the fight going out in them as well.

"Why do your tattoos do that—thing? I mean, why do they shine like that?" It's definitely a question she's been dying to ask, and Martin is the right person to answer it.

"They aren't tattoos, exactly. Think of them as…renewable energy. Each line, or bar, is a battery connected to our cells. Our weapons, some you've seen and many you haven't, rely on that electricity as a power source. But like any battery, they can run low, hence us training in this very room. The purple light acts the same as a power outlet, replacing the energy that is being used. We cannot afford to hone our skills and be left weakened—what if there is an attack? This way, we are constantly ready to fight if needed."

Completely fascinated, Eve only has more questions. "But Maggie said something about the Snappers being 'electric vampires.' How do your weapons, which are made of what they feed on, cause any real damage?"

Martin, evidently impressed by Eve's intelligence, is more than happy to continue. "Right you are. But how do you kill the unkillable? You can't drown, shoot, burn, or crush these mutations. They regenerate. The only way obliterate them is to overload their systems. Send high-voltage doses in a short period of time. By doing so, you explode their cells, quite literally turning them into dust."

"But what do you do if your batteries run out?" she asks, "If you're fighting a mutant, what then?"

Chills run up Eve's spine when Luca, behind her, whispers, "You run."

Pushing roughly past Eve and Martin, he heads down toward the mats, joining Beth and Rowan. Rolling her eyes, Eve tries to shake off her feelings of foreboding.

Spotting Maggie, Eve walks down the stairs and onto the mats. As she makes her way over, every voice within the arena grows silent. Face after face observes her, appraises her, judging the glasses-wearing newcomer.

Eve's cheeks blossom in embarrassment as she finally reaches Maggie, who, of course, is firmly planted next to West.

"Why is everybody staring?" Eve inquires, uncomfortable.

"Why do you think? Our parents are fucking traitors. Sorry to break it to you, Evie, but we're the black sheep of this joint."

"Eve, Maggie, come here, if you would?" Riley's booming voice beckons to the Abbott sisters. He still stands at the mouth of the tunnel leading back into the manor. Like a king observing his kingdom, the only things missing are a cape and a crown. Beth has joined him and offers them a friendly wave. Confused, the girls cautiously do as they are asked. Walking back across the mat, up the stairs, and into the tunnel once more.

They don't make it far before Riley abruptly stops. A single barcode-sized tattoo on his hand glows red, somehow unlocking a secret door. Unnerved, Eve watches as a rectangle of the stone wall lowers, exposing a brightly light room.

"Someone wants to be King Arthur!" Maggie snorts, noticing the round table and chairs in the center of the square space, the only items contained within. Eve and Maggie look to each other and hesitate before entering, wondering why there's such a need for privacy.

As if reading their minds, Riley pulls out a chair and sits, Beth doing the same. He motions for the Abbotts to join him, and they oblige.

"Don't worry, the door will stay open. I thought it best to have this conversation away from the others, as it needs to be had, and now."

"Whatever we've done wrong, it's Eve's fault," Maggie teases, hiding her concern.

"You're not in trouble. Well, you are, but not in the way that you think."

With that statement, Riley rises, the lights dim, and from the center of the table appears a hologram. Eve and Maggie are dumbfounded as something starts to play.

It is a recording. Looks to be within a warehouse, a bodycam of sorts. The wearer stealthily moves around a large machine and turns. Other fully outfitted Zappers are behind him, fanning out. He faces forward again, but instead of conveyor belts and machines, there are mutations as well. Eve counts six, identical to the level one from her bedroom in Saintsville. The warehouse fills slowly with their poisonous smoke.

But it's the two bodies in the very back, behind the monstrosities, that send a shiver down Eve's spine.

Adel and Orion.

Side by side.

The bodycam zooms in, and they both have lures around their necks.

The mutants start to hiss, and the camera-wearing Zapper looks up.

Clinging to the ceiling are countless more mutants. Packed so tightly together that they look like a writhing black cloud.

All at once, they let go.

Both Eve and Maggie scream as they fall, heading straight toward the camera as the feed turns to static.

Riley brings up the lights, and Eve and Maggie are crying.

"I'm sorry, but you have to see what we're up against."

Maggie rises and grabs her chair, flipping it to the ground.

Turning toward him, she screams, "Not that! We didn't need to see that! They're dead, right? They're all dead!"

"This footage was taken on our first attempt to bring them into custody. Your parents were the only survivors," Riley states gently.

Racking sobs have Eve on her feet in seconds, hugging her sister tightly to her.

"Yes, I am sorry, Maggie. I am so sorry…" mumbles Beth, soothingly. She has gotten to her feet as well, and cautiously approaches. Her role now apparent, Beth is there to provide additional moral support.

"It was important that you know that what the Quinns have informed you of is true. There has to be no doubt left for us to proceed."

Feeling Maggie calming, Eve releases her, and glares at Riley. In her mind, a warning of what they were about to watch would have been appropriate.

"Proceed? With what?"

"Joining us. We would like you to enlist in the EMTF."

Without hesitation, Maggie utters, "Where do I sign?"

"Maggie!" Eve exclaims.

"You saw! You saw what our parents did!"

"Yes, I saw, but let's take a moment!"

Everything is happening too fast. They have only just arrived, and now are being asked to make another life-altering decision. Eve agrees that her parents need to be brought to justice, but she also wants to protect Maggie in the process. If they do this, if they join them, there will be no turning back.

On the other hand, Eve also knows that wherever Maggie goes, whatever path, she will follow.

The path that Maggie had chosen was a foregone conclusion.

"Enough moments have been taken from us, Eve," Maggie roars.

Marching straight up to Riley would normally be comical, her being only half his height, but Maggie has that same "Beth" edge. When she means business, Maggie is a force of nature.

"Let's get the bastards."

Not waiting for Riley's response, she nods for Eve to follow her, as she walks straight out, and back into the dark tunnel.

Chapter 22

Eve and Maggie are officially enlisted members of the Electric Mutation Task Force, and Eve really has no clue what that fully means. There isn't a brochure or a website that she can visit and get an idea of what they are in for, not that she even could if she wanted to.

Irrational and upset, Eve and her sister signed on the dotted line without even reading their contracts very closely. Even mutant-hunting organizations have paperwork and legality issues, it seems.

As a minor, Maggie is still required to obtain her GED, but will be allowed to train and pick her studies via home-schooling at Evergreen in a year. Her disappointment is evident after hearing that West has already obtained his. It seems the youngest Quinn's brief appearance at Saintsville High was purely for show.

Their phones are taken away next by Riley. Eve is only allowed to shoot Jill a quick "We're safe, miss you, will be MIA for a bit" message before she is required to hand over her lifeline. Like any militaristic type training, minimal distractions are required to get maximum focus from cadets.

Do they call Zappers-in-training "cadets"? Sometimes Eve wishes she could just hit the off switch to her brain, and for a little while not have to speculate.

At least now the sisters have a clear direction of where they are headed, and a stipend to cover any extra expenses. Only when they're on "active duty" will they receive a full salary, according to Beth. She's been assigned by Riley as their point of contact, should any questions or complications arise.

Both Abbotts are more than okay with this arrangement. Beth, with her warm personality, has already provided them a welcome comfort. They're also issued more of the black clothing they've already been provided by the friendly older cook, who apparently is also in charge of inventory and apparel. Next, they're instructed to report to the underground ultraviolet training area in the morning.

For the rest of the day, neither sister discusses what they witnessed on that screen—not even later when they're all alone in their room. They don't need to discuss it…. Witnessing just one instance of their parents' brutality was enough. The Quinns have been telling the truth.

Day one in "the cave," as the other Zappers call it, isn't so bad. Mostly assessment and evaluation. Testing flexibility, muscle mass, and their current levels of fitness. Running, pushups, sit-ups, and more running, all while their vitals are recorded wirelessly into one of Martin's many contraptions.

But day two is when hell begins. Four in the morning, on the dot, Beth and Luca charge into Eve and Maggie's sleeping quarters, physically drag them out of bed, and bring them directly to the cave. No shower, no breakfast, though thankfully they are appropriately attired. Beth had warned them that their new uniform was to be worn at all times, including sleep.

Sent directly to the track around the edge, they are forced to run. Luca and Beth effortlessly maintain a brisk sprint, while Eve and Maggie keep falling pathetically behind. Only after their clothing is soaked and they feel like they can't move another inch does the fight training begin.

Eve, facing off against Beth, is slammed repeatedly to the floor. No matter how fast Eve is, Beth is faster.

"Don't be so sloppy! I can read every move before you even try to execute. Don't think so much, let your instincts take over!"

Trying to let go only seems to make things worse.

At nightfall, covered in bruises, the sisters crawl their way up the stairs and take turns soaking their sore muscles in the large tub.

Day three is more of the same. Early to rise, hours upon hours in the cave, and only a quick lunch and dinner. Eve takes to glaring at Riley when he pops his head in to observe, for he is the sadist that has ordered the Quinns to be in charge of their training. Beth isn't so bad—though she is giggly and sweet one moment and terrifying the next. Demanding, but patient, Eve can already see improvements in their fighting through her tutelage.

But Luca...Eve can't believe she had ever found that man appealing.

He does as he is ordered. Luca has no choice but to help in the training of the infamous daughters of Adel and Orion Abbott, and he doesn't let them forget it for a second. He likes the sound of his own voice, and he uses it to point out their every flaw. They would hinder every mission and be a liability in the field. At first, Eve thinks it's a training tactic, a cruel form of motivation, until Beth begins to speak up, mincing words with her beloved brother. Their relationship becoming strained by his ongoing behavior.

Day by day by day, they wake, train, then take their broken bodies to bed and start all over again.

The conditioning works.

Both Eve and Maggie are soon able to run flat out for over an hour, and spar for countless more beyond that. The boring, mindless repetition begins to translate into muscle memory. But while Maggie is excelling, Eve is falling more and more behind. It makes sense, really—Maggie, with her authority issues, thrives on Luca's belittling. It fuels and focuses her, while it rips Eve's confidence to shreds.

Eve wouldn't have mentally survived without their daily, private lessons with Martin.

They learn about the different kinds of mutants. Level ones are called smokers. The one that had attacked Eve in her bedroom had been a smoker, and the mildest form of the enemy they would soon face. Level two, fliers, are basically smokers with wings. Great, Eve thinks. Like those things need the ability to zip around in the air as well. Level three, jumpers. They couldn't fly, but they could leap twenty feet in the air and move faster than the first two, making them next to impossible to immobilize. And the fourth and final classified mutations are the rollers, the most advanced.

It takes five Zappers working together to take down one roller. Martin is their tutor during their daily "learn what you're up against" talks. Using holographs and projections, he replays footage from previous encounters, thankfully no more involving their parents, explaining in detail the strengths and weaknesses of their opponents.

And these are only the mutants the EMTF researchers have been able to closely study. Adel and Orion were apparently always hard at work, coming up with yet more genetic twists—providing Martin with endless material to teach his pupils.

Lesson by lesson, Eve's skin crawls, and her hatred for their parents and their part in all of this grows.

Before Adel and Orion's experiments, there had been only one kind of mutant. Smokers had been the only enemy. Now, they truly didn't know what they were up against or what twisted version of a former human would be popping up next.

A month passes before Eve finally feels herself getting stronger—before she ducks, rolls, and deflects more often than a foot or fist connects with her flesh. She is still behind her sister, but she is gaining a certain immunity to Luca's verbal attacks.

Many other fighters training in the arena agree with Luca's assessments. If he treats Eve and Maggie like outcasts, then they are going to follow his lead. The only living creatures that will say more than a few words to them—unless forced—are the Quinns, Riley, or the cook.

Things become even lonelier for Eve when she and Maggie are separated.

Since her sister graduated to instruction in weapons way before her, Eve steals every moment she can to watch Maggie off with Rowan. She isn't jealous of the ferocious little redhead. If anything, she is impressed by Maggie's quick comprehension of anything Rowan throws her way. Her little sister is calmer and more confident here. At Evergreen, Maggie is coming back to life again.

And Eve is pretty sure that her little sister is falling in love.

Two months into her training, Eve is awakened by another nightmare. This time, her father Orion had been injecting needle after needle into her limp body, strapped to an operating table. Each syringe that had been emptied into her veins causing her body to convulse and seize. Sobbing, she bolts up in bed, begging him to stop.

Looking from her bed to Maggie's, she notices that her sister's is empty—just a rumpled comforter with the pillows askew. The small clock on her nightstand reads midnight. Panicking, Eve hops out of bed, checks the bathroom, and then hurries over to the window, looking down onto the driveway illuminated by the moonlight. Frantically searching for movement, she notices what looks like someone in the hot springs. Cursing her near-sightedness, she grabs her glasses from her nightstand, running back to the window. Sure enough, there is a voluptuous ginger swimming in what seems to be her bra and underwear.

Maggie.

And she isn't alone. West, his baby face unmistakable, swims with Maggie to the waterfall as they both climb out onto the small ledge. It looks as if they are set to dive, racing each other back to the other side, when West grabs Maggie's wrist and straightens. Pulling her toward him, he takes his hands, cupping her cheeks, bending down to softly kiss her mouth.

Eve does not need to see that.

Backing away from the window, she feels like she's intruding. She just observed a steamy moment between two young adults and has no desire to witness what happens next.

But now Eve is wide awake. Fearing if she goes back to sleep, she will only fall back into her dreamscape, Eve puts on her boots and quietly makes her way downstairs. Before she knows it, her wanderings take her into the tunnel off the kitchen and back into the cave.

At this early hour, it is empty, smelling strongly of some sort of cleaning agent. She has noticed another entry to the right of the arena, with swinging double doors. Zappers frequently enter and exit throughout the day, but neither Eve nor Maggie have asked where it leads.

Her inquisitiveness getting the best of her, Eve looks over her shoulder and up at the many cameras on the walls. Whoever is currently stuck monitoring the security of this place hasn't stopped her yet, and she takes that as a sign that it is okay to proceed. Emboldened, she walks down the steps, over the mats, and up another set of stairs to the double doors.

Pausing before entering, she quietly pushes them open and steps through. Another tunnel sharply curves to the right, and a light source shines from somewhere around the corner. Cautiously approaching, she turns and sees a set of lockers and benches planted against the wall on either side. Also, two more doors. Checking each, Eve sees they lead to locker rooms which she assumes to be male and female (the obvious hint being the urinals in one).

Exiting the men's locker room, Eve explores the source of the light, a circular hole in the ceiling, last. Moving to stand right below it, she shields her eyes, and she notices metal rungs inserted in the cement wall. Evenly spaced, they had been installed purposefully, leading all the way up.

The rungs form a ladder.

She's gone this far already—there's no stopping her as she heads up and into the room in the ceiling. Her eyes are temporarily blinded by the intensity of the light. She is now in a round dome, every inch covered in small white bulbs.

Eyes watering from the intensity, she notices four more sets of benches in the center, and a man. Shirtless, he is only wearing a pair of loose-looking cotton shorts. His tattoos cover his muscled chest and legs, and they seem to pulse, drinking in the power of this place. Relaxed and laying across a bench in the middle, Eve is definitely intruding.

He looks up as she takes a step back, hearing her boots connecting with the floor. A pair of odd sunglasses are fitted over his chiseled, angular features.

Luca.

Chapter 23

"I am so sorry. I'm leaving...." Eve croaks, whipping back toward the ladder. Before she even takes a step, Luca quickly responds, "No...it's okay."

She freezes. Eve is used to rude, intolerable Luca. Not polite Luca.

"I was awake and went for a walk. Ended up down in the arena, and I was just wondering...." Eve speaks softly, embarrassed.

"This area isn't off limits. If it was, the doors would've been locked," Luca states, matter-of-factly. "You're in the recharge room. The lights in the training area help to maintain our energy levels, but in here, we can recover quicker if needed."

Luca rises, coming to his full height. He then maneuvers over to a white stand and picks up a pair of glasses identical to the ones he's wearing. Walking over to Eve, he hands them to her, and she accepts gratefully. Sliding them over her lenses, she breathes a sigh a relief. The strain on her eyes from the dome's intensity is grueling. It takes several seconds for the spots in her vision to clear.

Now, truly able to see Luca before her, Eve's stomach tightens. His chest and back are covered in the same barcoded designs as his arms, and they extend all the way down to his ankles. Each pulse, as they brighten and fade, is entrancing. She feels herself wanting to touch his skin. She wants to see if the tattoos are warm, or tingle under her fingertips. Luca lets her examine him, wordless and unabashed. She hasn't noticed before the small scars scattered across his limbs and strong body. Some white, old and healed, and others pink and still recuperating.

Realizing how creepy this must look, her slobbering over his half naked form, Eve blushes and starts to retreat.

"Wait, Eve, don't!" Luca rushes forward and grabs her arms, yanking her toward his chest, inches before she would have fallen down the circular entrance.

Stupid. Dumb. Eve always manages to feel inept in his presence. Looking up, she is about to whisper "thank you" until she realizes how close her face is to his. White teeth peek through his perfect lips. His eyes are unreadable, covered by the protective eyewear.

Eve is pretty sure that anything that adorned Luca would look sexy on his chiseled features.

He leans forward, coming even closer, until she can feel his hot breath pressing on her mouth. Luca smells like pine and peppermint. Heart pounding, blood racing with adrenaline, she thinks he's going to kiss her, but he pauses.

Slowly taking a step back, he releases her arms. After another pause, he walks away, depositing his glasses back into the basket. Refusing to look at her, Luca walks straight past and down the metal rung stairs.

Eve. Is. Mortified.

And she can't help but feel hurt. Plain as plain could be, Luca had an opportunity to initiate something with her. Her body language had been clear. If he was going to kiss her, she was all in. Instead, she had been rejected.

Ripping the glasses off, she tosses them, not caring how the rays pierce her irises. Eve just wants to get the heck out of this arena and back to the security of her assigned bedroom. Quickly climbing down the rungs, she skips the last four. Landing with a thud, Eve pivots, preparing to make a run for it when she sees Luca, now sitting on one of the benches outside the lockers.

He is still shirtless, his head in his hands, fingers massaging his scalp as he gently rocks back and forth. He's radiating frustration—evident from his body language.

Indignation fading to concern, Eve wants to ask him if he is okay when the door to the female locker rooms open. Walking out, with her hair damp and freshly washed body barely contained beneath a short towel, is Sophia.

For the past two months, she and her sister Lucia have treated Eve like she was a carrier of a life-threatening disease. Avoiding contact and conversation at all costs, she has not spoken to her since their first encounter.

"I'm ready to go again if you are…." Sophia purrs knowingly, her long legs glistening in the soft lighting.

Scratching the light stubble coating his jaw, Luca looks to Sophia, then seemingly remembers Eve.

His forehead wrinkles in concern, eyes locking with hers. Luca's about to speak when Eve shakes her head and walks straight past them. Almost to the double-doored exit, she stops, turning back to the obvious lovers.

Her words are directed at Luca.

"I was wondering why I wasn't learning anything from you in practice. Maybe if you spent less time fooling around, and more time actually trying, I might get better. Just a thought."

The smile on her features doesn't reach her cold eyes as Eve breaks away from the scene before her, numbly heading back toward her room.

When she peeks inside their moonlight-filled chambers, Maggie is back in her bed. Thinking her asleep, Eve tiptoes to her own mattress, the down comforter and luxurious sheets softly crinkling as she climbs beneath the covers. Laying her head gently on the soft pillow, she's about to close her eyes when she hears Maggie utter, "I'm sorry."

Rising to her elbows, she looks across the room.

"Sorry about what?" Eve questions.

Yawning, a sleepy Maggie mumbles, "I came back and you were gone. West showed me the control room, and we watched you guys on the security camera screens. Luca is a tool...."

Eves is humiliated once more.

"It looked like Captain Serious and you were gonna get it on...but you and Sophia, in one night? *Ew.* Be glad you didn't touch anything that has come in contact with that Zapper groupie."

Eve is touched by her baby sister coming to her defense. "You're right. I love you."

"Same. Now shut up, please, I'm tired...." Mumbling the last part, Maggie rolls onto her side, grabbing one of her pillows to hug. Within seconds, she is fast asleep.

Eve wants to sleep but can't. Tossing and turning, at some point during the early hours she must have dozed off, because the blaring of her alarm jars her awake.

Resentment.

She's sick and tired of all the hours she has wasted fighting her feelings toward Luca. Last night, everything became clear. He isn't worth it.

The odd hold he's had over her has been broken. Eve, for once, feels like she has nothing to prove.

Maggie can sense the storm clouds brewing. Her big sister is itching for a fight, and just waiting for the person who would give it to her first. Evergreen has been changing Eve as well, but Maggie doesn't know who her older sister is becoming.

The girls quickly brush their teeth and head through the kitchen, down the tunnel, and into the cave. They have gotten used to the various Zappers that come and go. Sometimes the training area is packed to the brim; other times, it's just the Quinns and the Abbotts. Beth always seems to be the first to arrive, this morning included. Warming up and stretching on one of the thick rubber mats, she appears to be watching a video on a tablet—the footage is shaky, obviously from a head cam.

Explosions, cries, movement. It appears to be a battle between a couple of Zappers and a massive hoard of fliers. Engrossed in the skirmish, Beth startles, realizing that Eve and Maggie are now standing before her. Deftly flipping the off switch, the tablet powers down, and she throws it into her backpack.

"Apologies, ladies, you weren't supposed to see that." Beth is sheepish and adorably sweet, concern marring her delicate features.

"There had to be at least a few hundred Snappers, Beth… was that real?" Maggie asks, flummoxed.

It takes a moment as the gorgeous blonde quickly calculates her answer. "Yes."

Eve and Maggie look to each other, their apprehension apparent.

"But I remember Martin saying in one of his never-ending lessons that fliers are rare, right? So then, how..." Maggie continues.

"How do you think?" Beth utters, bitterly.

Realization dawning on her, the youngest Abbott snarls, "Our parents seriously are the worst."

Eve hears footsteps as others join them. Without turning, she knows one of them is probably Luca. Looking over her shoulder, she sees him standing directly behind her. His gaze intense. Eve fills with rage as she glances at him, facing forward once more. A fury like nothing she has ever felt before has latched on, and she happily lets it consume her.

"What are you guys playing at? Day after day of training, more of the same, while you keep us in the dark about what is really going on out there. Has the world ended? Are we the last known survivors, holed up in this glamourous prison? Do you honestly think, after all that Maggie and I have gone through, that we can't handle the truth? Or are you too stupid to realize that we are smart enough to see straight through your bullshit?"

Beth's mouth drops open.

Eve is positively feral as she sneers at the group, stepping so that she is right in front of the female Quinn's face. Nodding calmly, Beth accepts the challenge. Raising her hands, she slowly starts to circle. Everyone but Eve and Beth pull back, giving the girls room to fight it out.

Round and round Beth goes, but Eve doesn't move. The tension thickens as the moments tick by, and the eldest Abbott remains motionless.

Tiring of Eve's inaction, Beth is ready to end this charade. Soundlessly, when her circle brings her to where Eve's back is facing her, she lunges—only for Eve to step aside at the last second. Beth rolls, coming to her feet, and whips back around. Now also raising her hands, Eve's eyes are untamed as she ignores the whistling and catcalls.

Both girls start to circle.

Maggie, honestly, hadn't thought Eve had it in her.

Gone is her insecure, awkward older sister. The woman before her is terrifying. Her kicks, punches, moves, and counter-moves coming so fast that Maggie has a hard time following. All that she knows is—Eve is winning.

A crack of Eve's elbow into Beth's nose, and a side kick to her stomach knocks the wind straight out of her. Merciless, another front kick, and low roundhouse sends Beth flying onto her back.

Eve is on top of Beth, her hands firmly around her neck, choking her. Blood flows from Beth's nose as her face darkens. Her right hand claws at Eve's strong grip, then flies to the mat, repeatedly slapping the surface. Beth has surrendered, but Eve isn't letting go.

There's a commotion, as it takes both Rowan and Tate to peel Eve off, kicking and screaming, as their baby sister coughs and gasps. And then, Beth is laughing. Hoarse, her vocal cords raw and already swelling, she only laughs louder, unable to control her tear ducts flowing in response. Wiping her eyes, Beth watches as Eve struggles to break free from Rowan and Tate, calling them names that have even Maggie impressed.

"I think…they are both ready…to get inked…." Beth cackles, finding the entire debacle hysterical.

At this, Eve stills. Her fury replaced with confusion.

"We're going to get power strips implanted?" Eve inquires cautiously.

"Duh! How else are you going to leverage one of the rusty old weapons in this place! The only question is…which one of us is going to have to honor of escorting you?"

As if on cue, Luca moves to stand in front of Eve as she is freed by Rowan and Tate. Everyone in the room watches her, making sure she doesn't head straight back at Beth.

"I'll do it," Luca volunteers.

"You?" It's Eve's turn to laugh. "Absolutely not!"

Surveying the group, Eve storms from the room, not looking back once.

Chapter 24

She walks straight out the front door, her boots crunching on the gravel driveway. Eve can't stay in that house for one more second. Part of her wants to starting running and never stop. Another part wants to march back inside and fight every inhabitant one by one.

Eve no longer recognizes the woman standing with blood on her hands. She is rougher, less forgiving. Like the jagged stones beneath her soles. The more she is pushed and pushed, the more she finds herself wanting to push back. Here at Evergreen, she has never been more unhappy.

It isn't just Luca.

This place has turned her into a killer, just like them.

Before, she was kind, quiet, gentle. What she has just done to Beth in there makes her feel tainted. She felt the bones break in Beth's nose when her elbow had connected. And, in that moment, it felt good.

But now there is only shame. Fighting is addicting—inflicting pain creates a sort of high. Eve now understands why professional boxers allow their bodies to be pummeled over and over.

Because they enjoy it.

Spotting the hot springs, empty and bubbling right in front of her, she doesn't hesitate.

Stripping down to her sports bra and high-cut briefs, Eve cautiously steps into the steamy pool. Bruises new and old litter her pale skin. She wonders why she hasn't done this before as the heat relaxes her aching muscles. Speaking of musculature, that change is new as well. Physically, Eve is starting to look like any one of the mutant hunters, cut and defined, even though she knows that they will never truly accept her.

Even when she is tattooed and battle proven, she and Maggie will always be outsiders.

Swimming off to the side and facing away from the log mansion, the sun has almost set as she rests her head on her hands. Observing the swaying grass in the field and the trees that border it, Eve hears a singular pair of boots approaching.

It has to be close to seven—the time when they're usually dismissed and allowed to grab a quick meal before retiring for the evening. Clenching her jaw, she refuses to acknowledge whomever the intruder might be, having made it quite clear that she wants to be left alone.

Splash. A body dives in, sending a wave of soothing water higher up Eve's back before it settles.

That same someone comes up for air, disturbing the surface as they swim their way over, joining Eve at the wall.

"You're cute when you're pouting," Rowan drawls.

Of all the people Eve expected it to be, Rowan was toward the bottom of the list.

Since their time in Saintsville together, Eve really hasn't had much contact with him. Besides stealing glances of Rowan's sessions with Maggie, they both have been doing their own thing. She knows that most of the Quinns do not spend all their time at this base. Many disappear for days at a time, on whatever mission Riley deems appropriate.

A fresh scar and stitches sit directly above his left eye. From the angry look of his flesh surrounding the wound, it was definitely Snapper inflicted.

The good thing about Rowan, Eve ponders, it that she doesn't lean one way or the other with him.

She doesn't hate him, and she isn't fond of him either. He is just a smooth-talking stranger, and probably one of the few people she doesn't mind being next to at the moment.

Because honestly, when it comes to Rowan, she just doesn't care.

"Nice shorts," Eve mumbles sarcastically, noticing the orange, Hawaiian-print swim trunks he has brought out for the occasion.

"Shh, they're contraband. If Riley spots me in anything but, 'EMTF-approved articles of clothing,' I will get spanked."

"You mean something other than black?"

"Correct, solider. You will obey, am I making myself clear?" So perfect is Rowan's impersonation of Riley that Eve bursts out laughing.

"You're weird," Eve smirks, her mood lightening.

Friends. She and Rowan can be friends.

Eve didn't realize how much she needed a friend, and at the moment, she can't afford to be picky.

Seeing the mischievous twinkle in his eyes as he splashes water at her exposed head, her mind is changed once again. New potential friendship with someone who is attractive, ripped, and has cool hair?

Eve could do worse.

Chapter 25

At Rowan's suggestion, Eve meets him at the crack of dawn outside the compound. Her breath is visible as a gentle mist rolls on the ground. Half awake, she yawns, tucking her cold hands under her arms. Eve regrets not wearing a windbreaker over her hoodie, but Rowan promised her a run.

Sure enough, right at five o'clock, he comes bouncing down the stairs in sweatpants and a hoodie identical to hers. Bright and chipper, Eve grimaces. Rowan appears to be well rested, while Eve is bone weary.

Last night had gifted her another nightmare. Worms had been crawling under her skin, and no matter how much she had clawed, she couldn't get them out. Waking up in another panic, her throbbing arms were covered in deep, self-inflicted scratches.

She thinks maybe it's time to talk to someone about the dreams. But the only person she trusts is her sister, and her sister isn't exactly the most empathic person on the planet.

Plus, Maggie is spending more and more time with West. According to her sibling, they aren't "official" and she doesn't "believe in commitment," but Eve can see plain as day that Maggie is lying to herself if she thinks she would be happy with anyone else.

As Rowan approaches, the corners of his eyes crinkle slightly in concern. Eve realizes she must look as bad as she feels.

"Hey...you okay?" Rowan inquires, studying her.

"Yes. I'm fine. Ready?"

"If you get tired at all, let me know, we can do intervals of walking and running."

"Rowan, let's just go...."

Pulling her hood up over her head, Eve starts to jog down the driveway with Rowan quickly catching up. But he isn't done talking.

"How far do you want to go? Riley has already given his approval. We can skip endurance training, as long as we are back by breakfast. But it's up to you...."

His words stagnate as they warm up, their pace increasing.

"I want to be gone for as long as we are allowed."

He nods, and it only takes a few minutes before they reach the main gate. Whoever is stationed at the surveillance cameras—still a mystery to Eve—scans them, and then lets them through.

For the first time in months, Eve is beyond Evergreen's walls and out in the open. Sweat trickles down her back and between her breasts, soaking her tank top beneath her hoodie. Letting Rowan take the lead, he brings them to a thin trail in the heavy woods, and the terrain changes, carrying them up the side of a steep hill.

Her legs burn and her heart pounds against her ribcage before she finally surrenders, slowing to a walking pace. She doesn't know if this is sad or not, but this simple run is turning into the most fun she has had in a while.

Rowan, realizing that Eve is no longer pacing him, walks back down the hill to join her. Having long since removed his hoodie and tank top, tying them to his waist, his bare skin is flushed.

"You...quit on me!" he says between labored breaths, using his forearm to remove the sweat sliding down his cheeks. "Come on, woman...you got more in you!"

"I don't do hills...." Eve wheezes, laughing.

Rowan joins her and they continue to climb all the way up. When they arrive at the top, the view is well worth it.

Dark blue water extends for what must be miles, reflecting the mountains in the distance. A giant lake rests before them, undisturbed except by the fish touching the surface. They watch as a group of birds dips down for a drink. Feeling overheated and longing to feel the breeze on her skin, Eve peels off her hoodie and walks over to a large, flat outcropping of rock. Sitting down, Rowan joins her.

A sharp intake of breath, and then warm hands gently grab her left forearm. Rowan raises it, surveying the damage. Mentally kicking herself, Eve realizes she had forgotten about her arms.

"Eve...what happened?"

Instantly defensive, she yanks her wrist free. Grabbing her hoodie, Eve throws it back on and goes to stand, but Rowan delicately tugs her back to the ground. All it takes is looking into his gentle brown eyes, and Eve bursts into tears.

Before she knows it, Rowan is hugging her, his big hands rubbing her back.

"It's okay...shh. It's gonna be okay."

He lets her cry until there is nothing left.

Leaning away from him, she uses her sleeves to blot her face, turning toward the lake.

"Did you…do that to yourself?" Rowan proceeds cautiously, his voice strained.

"No! Yes, but…not what you think. It's complicated…." Eve mumbles, her head starting to throb from an impending headache.

"Then uncomplicate things."

"You're not going to believe me."

"I work for a secret government agency, tracking and destroying human mutations caused by their systems being over-loaded with electrical currents. I think I can probably keep an open mind, especially when it comes to you…." Rowan is back to being an obnoxious flirt, but she can tell he is still distressed.

"I didn't know I was doing this when it happened. I was having a dream…."

"Damn, girl. S&M-style or…"

"Rowan! Ugh, you're as bad as Maggie!"

"Apologies, continue."

And after a deep breath, she does. Once Eve starts talking, the words pour out of her. How the nightmares started after her parents went missing. How they are steadily becoming more vivid. The odd correlations between them—like dreaming glass was embedded in her palm and waking to find a scar she hadn't noticed before.

She talks about not fitting in. Not in the real world. Not in the Quinns' world. Not ever, really. She talks and talks, confiding everything to him and the lake. When she's done, she looks over to Rowan—deep in thought. Scratching the stubble on his chain, he sighs and stands, offering a hand that Eve accepts. Lifting her to her feet, she picks a few pine needles from her pants, waiting for his response.

"When I said 'we should go running,' I had no idea that it would turn into therapy hour…" Rowan teases.

"I should have known," Eve accuses, her cheeks heating.

"Don't worry, baby girl, I won't tell any of my nosey family members what you just told me. But I would be lying if I didn't say that I was concerned...."

They start to move, hiking back down the hill.

"Well, what do you think is wrong with me?"

Rowan gives her a knowing look before saying, "A lot of things."

"Can you be serious, please?" Eve begs, needing him to focus.

Sobering, Rowan rubs his palms together.

"I think that all of this might be a sort of stress response? First your parents, then having to take care of Maggie. And we stepped into the picture and further muddied everything. You're super uptight in general, no, don't shake your head, you know I'm right. I think that your body is trying to put all that energy into something."

Eve can tell that Rowan isn't totally convinced, but what he is saying isn't something Eve hasn't already thought of herself.

"But how do I stop the dreams? Drugs? Do I need to be restrained? I am so tired...."

"Don't worry, we will figure it out."

Throwing a friendly arm around her shoulder, he gives it a squeeze before breaking back into a jog.

"You coming? We're going to be late!" he yells, over his shoulder.

"Late for what?" she questions.

Wiggling his eyebrows, he yells back, "You'll see!"

Chapter 26

Riley is waiting on a leather couch just inside the entrance, his left foot tapping in annoyance. Eyes narrowing, he wordlessly reprimands Rowan for their tardiness. The mischievous Quinn just points to Eve and shrugs playfully.

She is instructed by their leader to grab a quick shower, some breakfast, and meet him back here in one hour.

Paying the price for her hard run, each step Eve takes up the three flights of stairs to her room is laborious. Stopping on the third-floor landing for a moment, she needs a break to continue. Four doors down from Eve and Maggie's dorm is another door with a fish carved on the front. It looks to be a salmon, and as it opens, Sophia and Lucia step out.

Eve really does have the worst luck.

Painfully straightening, she moves to the side so they can pass, keeping her eyes diverted.

Heavy perfume accosts her as the girls approach, but thankfully they don't engage. Eve hears them whispering as they descend to the second level, and then the first.

"I seriously can't stand her."

"She's a total psycho. You saw her on the mats yesterday, right?"

"Dumb luck. Beth was having an off day...."

Eve chooses not to listen to the rest as she limps to her bedroom, showers, and changes into her usual uniform. Ignoring literally everyone at breakfast except Rowan, she meets Riley back in the lobby at exactly nine.

The smile on his face falls when he notices the scabs her nails have inflicted on her arms, but Riley doesn't ask any questions.

All business all the time, he gets right to the point.

"As you may or may not know, we've been doing our very best to cram what usually takes years into weeks. Thankfully, your martial arts backgrounds have given you and Maggie a solid foundation. I've been impressed by the progress and dedication from you both."

Eve hadn't heard Maggie approach, but now she's standing beside her. Her wild, red curls are loose and in peak form. Bits of yellow-and-gold highlights are starting to show through, undoubtedly from her time sneaking around outside with a certain Quinn. Riley's speech continues as Maggie eyes Eve's arms, mouthing, "Ouch...."

"Later," Eve mouths back as Riley stops speaking, realizing the girls are no longer listening.

When they're both refocused on him, he continues.

"We can only teach you so much theory, but you will learn the most from experience. That being said, Beth and the other instructors think you're both ready to fully shift your focus to weapons training. Maggie, you have had a bit of a head start with Rowan, but Eve, I have faith you will catch on quickly. We need to see what in our arsenal best suits your particular abilities—"

"Yes! We are getting tattooed!" Maggie interrupts. "You can put them anywhere, and I mean *anywhere*, and I won't say a word…."

Smirking, Eve tries not to laugh at the appalled look on Riley's face. Her time with Rowan has helped to lighten her mood.

"That is correct," Riley answers, straight-faced. "If you will follow me, please."

Eve and Maggie accompany Rowan back toward the dormitories, but instead of heading up, they walk across the flagstone and toward a large glass window, looking upon another beautiful grass field.

He stops a good ten feet from the window, and a grating sound reveals a thin white pole rising from the floor. A small camera, like the ones at the gate, scans Riley from head to toe before freezing and returning to where it was hidden beneath a stone tile.

The Abbott sisters aren't surprised when the wall looking outwards starts to push forward, stops, then rotates on an axis until it is parallel to them—revealing a hidden tunnel.

"How many of those mystery doors do you have, boss?" Maggie inquires. Riley again, doesn't respond.

The field is just footage playing on an intense high-tech screen—a live feed from a camera placed outside on the back of Evergreen mansion.

Eve can't help but walk around and look out the "window" again, before proceeding down the tunnel with Maggie and the owner of this complex home. Even from up close, there was no pixelation or indication that it was anything but a window looking out onto a field.

"You people sure have a flair for the dramatic," Maggie states sarcastically. Eve can tell that she's impressed, but her sister always needs to play the "cool card."

"There is a need for secrecy," Riley retorts.

"And what might that be?"

"Only a billion dollars' worth of technology, and the ability to weaponize anyone who gets their hands on it."

"Well...when you put it that way, hidden tunnels it is!"

Once they step past the false window and into the chamber, the door rotates back until it shuts. They hear a loud click as mechanisms within it slide, locking them inside.

With Riley as their tunnel tour guide, they first pass a control room. The girls only spare a quick glance through the transparent walls and door. The glass is so thick, Eve guesses it has to be bulletproof. Several screens cover the walls in a semicircle, illustrating just how little privacy they've had all along.

A man with silver hair, who Eve has seen briefly before in the cave, is seated in a chair in the middle. His body is anything but relaxed as his eyes flick from one screen to the next, checking for anything that might be out of the ordinary.

Maggie notices one particular camera view angled on the hot springs out front and gives Eve a knowing look. Not that Maggie really cares, but she'll be more discreet in her rendezvous from now on.

"Is this where you and West saw Luca and I...?" Eve whispers, referring to the night that West and Maggie had observed Luca almost kissing her in the recharge room.

"Oh, no! There is another hidey-hole in the dormitories with monitors. Can honestly say, I haven't been in here before," Maggie explains, also whispering. Not that it does any good, their words inadvertently echoing in the tunnel.

Coming to stop, there is a thick, gunmetal gray door. Another camera, another quick scan of Riley before it slides to the right, exposing the white laboratory before them.

Martin is tinkering with some screens on the wall, and Eve can tell instantly that this is his happy place. He loads some sort of program and a solid form of a woman appears. Swiping, he sends the image to a screen in the center. Other numbers, graphs, and dials are present on multiple surfaces everywhere she looks.

Eve's palms are sweating. Her ears aren't even pierced. She can feel her adrenaline starting to surge.

Squatting on the ground, a certain someone has a soft gray cloth and is cleaning multiple cameras arranged in the shape of a circle on the floor. He looks up, and Eve flusters.

Avoiding Luca isn't going to be as easy as she thought.

Her delicate enthusiasm crumbles.

Looking to the ceiling in frustration, Eve tries not to cause a scene…even though she wants to whine and stomp her feet until he finally leaves.

Just his presence is going to ruin what she thinks is a special rite of passage.

The Abbotts have worked hard to earn these purpose-driven tattoos. Burying her feeling, Eve will scream later, but she isn't going to let her frustration spoil this moment for Maggie.

Spotting the sisters, Luca heads towards them, slapping the towel he is holding over his shoulder. He, too, notices Eve's scratched arms as she crosses them in front of her chest.

Thankfully, he says nothing.

Riley breaks the tension, clapping his hands together and exclaiming, "Who wants to go first?"

The words barely leave his lips before Maggie's hand shoots into the air.

"I am ready to be desecrated," she positively purrs.

With a small bow, Riley steps back, and leaves them alone with the Quinns in the laboratory. Eve has never felt claustrophobic before now. Sweat starts to bead on her forehead as she tries not to think of her nightmares. The things she dreamed had been done to her in a lab—similar to this one. For some reason, Rowan and the lake pop into her thoughts. The dark blue water. The birds. She starts to replay the good parts of her morning like a ticker reel in her mind, and it works. Her tension starts to ease.

Martin runs Maggie through a series of standard questions.

"Do you want privacy during the procedure?"

"Nope."

"Do you have any sensitives to pain medications that we should be aware of?"

"Thankfully not! Drug me up!" Maggie claps her hands together in excitement.

Satisfied, Martin instructs Maggie to remove everything but her bra and underwear.

You don't have to ask Maggie to get semi-naked twice.

Unselfconsciously stripping down, she waits for further instructions, leaving Maggie in just the standard-issue sports bra and underwear. Martin can't help but take in her killer curves as he coughs, his neck reddening. Eve finds it comical, as Maggie raises her arms and stretches, knowing exactly the effect she is having on him.

Poor guy.

Turning quickly away, Martin asks her to step into the center of the cameras but to make sure not to come in contact. Any dust or smudges would interfere in the process.

"We need to back up," Luca commands, putting his arm in front of Eve and herding her toward the wall.

Spotting a few metal chairs, Eve takes one, moving it over so she can still watch Maggie but not have to be next to Luca.

Grabbing the other chair, Luca brings it next to hers and sits down, pretending he doesn't notice what she's attempting.

The lighting in the room dims as Martin instructs the youngest Abbott to stand with her legs spread, arms out wide. The cameras in the center start to lift out of the concrete. Thousands of tiny red lasers begin at her toes and rise until they pass her head, completing a full body scan.

"Can we talk?" Luca inquires carefully.

"Now? About what?" Eve snaps.

Another machine from the ceiling is giving Maggie a sort of spray tan…but instead of delivering a summer glow, she's being sterilized and administered a topical numbing agent.

"You know what."

Eve looks at Luca. His knee is brushing hers. Between the anticipation for what is about to happen to Maggie and herself, and any sort of physical contact, she is having a hard time thinking straight.

"Say what you need to say, and then get the hell away from me."

Eve doesn't know if she wants to hit him or kiss him.

"Nothing happened between Sophia and I," he states. Luca is actually nervous. "We were literally sparring, that's it. She was saying she was ready to 'go again,' as in she was recharged enough for another round."

He bites his lower lip, and the intensity of his gaze causes Eve's breath to catch.

"Oh."

Turning her head away in an attempt to hide her mortification, she checks in on Maggie. Martin has mapped out the placement and locations of her battery strips, utilizing the 3D render from the cameras. For now, she would just be getting them on her arms, from the wrist line to the top of her shoulders.

Luca's hand moves to rest on her knee. The heat it emanates is almost unbearable.

"But in the dome. I thought you were going to…" Eve swallows. "But you backed away. I received the message, loud and clear. Not interested. You don't owe me any explanations."

Luca leans in further.

"It's complicated," he whispers.

The lights in the room start to brighten once more, and that's Luca's cue to remove his hand and slide away, turning to face toward Maggie.

He was an absolutely horrible human being to her during training, then almost kisses her, and now puts his hand on her knee and tells her that "it's complicated"? Luca and Eve aren't even in a relationship, and it's already toxic.

"The dome will lower. Hold completely still. First, the skin grafts will be applied, then the solar cells. Followed by another graft. The whole process takes less than two minutes."

Nodding that she understands to Martin, Maggie searches until she finds Eve's face and winks. A solid silver chamber descends until it makes contact with the concrete, hiding Eve's beautiful sister from view. For Eve, the two minutes feel like two hours before the dome starts to rise.

Her baby sister's form starts to come into view. Maggie's toned calves. Strong thighs. As it reaches her waist, Eve can start to make out her arms. Lines, upon lines, upon lines. The surrounding skin is pink and affronted. But Maggie is positively glowing as her new appearance is revealed.

"Martin, you're the man!" Maggie exclaims, inspecting her new barcoded epidermis. Satisfied, she yells at her sister, "Eve, get over here! You're up."

The eldest Abbott's knees start to buckle as she stands, anxiety rearing its ugly head.

Maggie is getting dressed—like what has just occurred is the most natural thing in the world—and giving Martin a final show in the process.

Only then does Eve realize that she too will be asked to strip down...that is, if she agrees to proceed.

"Eve, do you want privacy during the procedure?"

She swallows before answering Martin, "No..."

He asks the same medical and consensual questions he had just rattled off to Maggie, with an additional one.

"Do you desire your vision to be restored to twenty-twenty while undergoing the solar cell implementation?"

"What?" Eve gasps.

"She does! Martin, she does! Yeah, bitch!" yells Maggie, now occupying Eve's chair next to Luca.

Her declining vision, among other things, has been causing frequent headaches from the eyestrain alone. If Martin could fix it, she would gladly accept.

"You can do that?"

"I can do more than that," he retorts.

Indicating Martin's face—with the lenses firmly in place—she can't help but ask, "Then...why haven't you fixed your vision?"

Martin takes off his glasses, offering them to Eve for her to inspect. "My eyesight has been perfect for some time. They're now merely a tool."

Holding them up to her own, she can make out numbers, statistics, and screens interacting with the gadgets being used within the laboratory. Fearing that this particular pair of spectacles cost more than she will make in her lifetime, Eve gingerly hands them back.

"If you will please remove everything but your undergarments and head to the center, we can proceed."

Eve hesitates and turns her back to everyone. Her hands shake as she slowly peels off her tank top, placing it on a stool. She does the same with her shoes, socks and lastly, pants.

"It only feels like your skin is being burned off for the first minute!" Maggie yells, messing with her.

Finally, gingerly stepping over the cameras, she comes to the center and wrenches herself to face forward—in plain view of Maggie and Luca. She can tell that her baby sister is proud of her, as she gives her two cheesy thumbs up. But her stomach twists when she locks eyes with Luca.

Like the cameras, he slowly scans her exposed flesh up and down. And the expression on his face causes her to pull her shoulders back.

He might as well take a good look, because this is never happening again.

Chapter 27

Removing her glasses last and handing them to Martin, Eve's world goes slightly out of focus. Arms out, sterilized and numbed, the chamber lowers. She is left standing alone inside the metal tube.

Martin has assured her that even with her "injuries" she can still take part in her first session. If anything, the grafts will help to speed up the healing process, kicking her body into overdrive.

Closing her eyes, she tries to remain calm. The intense feeling of déjà vu further complicating matters. She hears Martin's voice coming through some sort of speaker in the ceiling.

"Okay, Eve, hold perfectly still. This shouldn't hurt, but if it does, any movement will cause the program to immediately stop. Do I have your permission to proceed?"

Her voice cracks as she whispers, "Yes."

Eve's arms warm as the whirring of machines move within the space. Her heart pounds, adrenaline kicking in.

Heat.

She refuses to look, squeezing her eyes closed. A minute has to have already passed—she just has to make it one more.

A cold, tingling sensation comes next. Probably due to the solar cells being inserted, but that means she is almost there. Heat again, indicating the second skin graft, securing the battery packs in place.

"Eve, I'm ready for your eyes. Can you look straight ahead, please, focusing on the blue dot in the center? Don't move."

Forced to open, she spares a quick glance at both of her arms, before Martin repeats, "Blue dot, please...."

Following his orders, she looks to the metal wall. A small blue light has appeared. She doesn't see, but hears a contraption emerging from the side of the wall. It looks like a set of goggles as it comes into view, lining up directly in front of her face. Pausing, it moves forward until it rest against Eve's cheekbones.

"Nice and wide, and three, two...."

One.

She feels her eyeballs getting zapped. Only way to explain it. There's a slight sting as she's forced to blink, tears running down her cheeks in response to the trauma.

The cylinder starts to raise as everything slowly comes into focus. Sharp and crisp, Eve feels like she's been living her entire life in black and white. The small cracks in the concrete floor jump out at her, unable to see them prior to this magic.

And her new tattoos are unnerving. Placed with such precision, the overall result is intimidating. She feels stronger because of them. They're one more tool that she is going to need if she is ever going to be allowed to do any real good.

Old Eve would have *never* gotten a tattoo. New Eve now has too many to count.

Maggie starts whistling and cat calling. Sheepish, Eve hurriedly throws her clothes back on, her arms stinging from the contact with fabric. The topical numbing cream, while extremely effective, is wearing off fast. Thanking Martin, she heads over to Maggie and Luca, unsure of what happens next.

"No glasses, some ink. Miss Abbott, you might actually be cool!" the youngest Abbott exclaims.

Maggie holds out her arms, comparing the designs on hers to Eve's. Luca approaches as well, and takes Eve's left wrist, carefully turning it from side to side.

"Martin, I think you screwed up on this section," Luca informs. "Everything is off center."

Eve sucks in air, her features horrified as she snaps her head toward Martin.

"Ignore him. No errors were made." Engrossed in his tablet, Martin's response is bored as he types away. Luca smirks.

"Well, what Eve said! What now?" Maggie inquires, looking to Luca for answers.

"Now, go and rest. Beth will come by this afternoon with further instructions." Martin politely dismisses them, his work done.

The thick airlock opens, letting them exit the laboratory. Maggie flashes Eve a knowing grin and strolls out first, leaving her older sister alone with the oldest Quinn. Side by side, Eve and Luca stroll, but neither of them speaks. It isn't uncomfortable; if anything, it's oddly peaceful.

They have been at war with each other since the first day they met, and finally, someone has won. The question is *who*.

Stepping out of the tunnel and back into the dormitories, Luca quickly departs. Heading, more than likely, to some Riley-appointed task in the cave. Too jazzed from what they've just experienced, the sisters make their way to their room. As soon as the door shuts, they burst into conversation.

"It didn't hurt at all. I was so scared!" Eve blurts.

"Right? The tube thing was a bit much. They could at least add a window or something," Maggie adds, throwing herself onto her bed. The moments she lands, the redhead howls in pain, forgetting her very tender new accessories.

"Fucking motherfucker!"

Eve can't help herself. Unable to hold back her giggles, she erupts in laughter.

"Shut up," Maggie grumbles, holding her arms out in front of her and blowing, trying to cool the angry red skin surrounding her barcodes.

"I'm sorry, I am so sorry! Are you okay…" she says, but she only laughs harder.

Eve suddenly realizes—she feels happy. Today, she has solidified a friendship with Rowan, come to some sort of cease-fire with Luca, and shared a bonding moment with Maggie in the lab.

It is amazing how one day can change everything.

Maggie twists her zombie, outstretched limbs toward her, gets off her bed, and before Eve knows it—she's being hugged.

"Thank you. I…I don't know if I have ever thanked you," Maggie says, "for all that you have done for me. I'm an asshole a lot, but I do love you."

Eve's laughter turns to tears, and the dampness on her shoulder lets her know that Maggie is crying as well. Both climbing onto Maggie's four-poster, the girls lose track of time as they talk and reminisce, and before long, fall fast asleep.

A sharp knock, and Eve looks for her alarm clock—but it's not there. She realizes that she's still in Maggie's bed. A bowl of popcorn they smuggled from the kitchen has tipped, blending in with the already-white comforter. Finally locating Maggie's timepiece, it reads 7:00 p.m.

The handle slowly turns and Beth's lovely face peeks from around the corner. Martin must have administered something to her Eve-inflicted injuries from the day prior, because all evidence of the eldest Abbott's assault has vanished. Beth's beautiful features are back to their glorious state.

Maggie is still out cold. That girl could sleep through a freight train.

"Hey. How you feeling?" Beth whispers.

"Not bad, but my arms are really sore. But that's normal, right?"

Eve's arms are itchy and slightly irritated. Not unbearable, but not comfortable either.

"Yup. Just wait until they do your chest if you think this is bad…" Beth giggles, and then asks shyly, "Can you come with me for a second?"

Based on the twinkle in her eye, Eve can tell that Beth is up to something.

"Yeah, hold on…."

Locating her socks and boots, Eve slips them on, joining the bubbly Quinn in the hallway.

"So, we usually have this thing that we do after first sessions. A…celebration of sorts? But it dawned on me that you and Maggie have nothing to wear."

Beth motions for her to follow as they head down to the second level, coming upon a door with a pinecone expertly carved into the exterior.

"Kindly enter my chambers!" Throwing the door open grandiosely, Beth bows, motioning for Eve to go first.

This side is Eve's favorite side of Beth. The sweet, charismatic best-friend type. Her hair is once again down and soft, her loose shiny curls enough to make any girl envious.

Entering Beth's room, it's exactly the same as Eve and Maggie's. The eldest Abbott is slightly disappointed, expecting her to have a television or hipper furniture. Beth seems to be able to get away with the most when it comes to the rules—Riley and everyone else have a soft spot for her.

"I know what you're thinking—boring. But I rarely spend time in here anyways. I'm always pestering one of my annoying brothers. That being said, what I lack in decorations, I make up for in clothes. Oh, and I also have an encrypted satellite phone. Riley looks the other way, because your girl here has an online shopping addiction! Thank you, United States government for cutting me a fat check every month. And I also know what you're thinking—I pick up my packages once a month in town, which is a gazillion miles away. But worth it, because the postal clerk is actually hella fine…."

Beth rambles as she stands in front of the door to her closet. When she finally opens it and flips on a light, Eve once again bursts out laughing.

Every single inch is covered in shoeboxes, purses, designer outfits, belts, and numerous hats.

Beth is an adorable hoarder.

"You need an intervention," Eve teases.

"Right? But clothes make me happy, and I make everyone else happy, so what's a girl to do?"

The gorgeous blonde starts pulling various dresses and holding them up to Eve. The ones she likes she tosses on her bed, the others she throws into a pile on the floor.

A perplexed Eve asks, "What are you doing?"

"Didn't you hear the part about a celebration? *We* are celebrating. *You* can't wear what you are wearing to where we are going. And I hope to God I have something that will fit Maggie in this mess."

"Where are we going?!"

"Somewhere that is not here…."

To Eve, "not here" sounds really, really good.

Chapter 28

"I hate mascara," Eve complains.

The Abbott sisters have become Beth's dolls.

Finding out that they are actually leaving the compound for a bit, Eve barrels upstairs and jumps on Maggie's bed until she has no choice but to acknowledge her.

All it takes is Eve saying two words.

Boys. Party.

And Maggie is wide awake.

Thankfully Beth does find a couple of dresses that will contain Maggie's robust cleavage, and soon both girls are submitting to beauty makeovers. Thankfully, they are in good hands. It just takes looking at Beth to know that she is an artist.

Two hours later, between outfit selection, hair styling, and glitter liquid liner, all three girls are finally ready.

West checks in a few times, anxious to get going. But Eve just knows it's an excuse to stare at Maggie. Her sister selects an orange, beaded minidress. It fits her like a glove, and Eve has never seen her more radiant.

Bubbly Beth has taken Maggie's wild curls and smoothed them into a French twist, adding some clips on one side for *pop*. Her black winged liner and smoky eye complete Maggie's transformation.

On the other hand, Eve isn't sure about her new look. Fastening her silver heels, she studies her reflection in a full-length mirror hanging in Beth's cramped closet.

The dress she's sporting is not her first choice. For one, it's long and dark blue, which is fantastic, but the high slit up the side that comes to right below her derriere is a bit too risqué. Long sleeves with a high neckline, the back is completely open to her waist. Beth had pulled her hair into a low, messy bun and given her bangs a trim. She'd kept her makeup subtle: mascara and a bit of clear gloss, with blush to top things off.

While Eve's outfit is sexy to the max, her makeup and hair is sweet and innocent.

Joining her at the mirror, Beth is rocking a rainbow jumpsuit with eyeshadow to match. Keeping her hair down, long and loose, she looks like a disco goddess.

"Are you sure I look okay?" Eve questions, nervous.

"Ha. Let's just see what my brothers think. Their reactions are going to be priceless."

Squealing, Beth grabs her hand and then Maggie's, dragging them out of her room.

Heading across the foyer and out the front entrance, when the girls arrive at the driveway, a string of black Humvees is already lined up.

Apparently, quite a few Zappers are joining in tonight's excursion.

Tate, Martin, Rowan, Luca, and West are talking in a circle. And for the first time since they have met, Eve and Maggie are seeing them in something other than black. All of the brothers have on various dress shirts and jeans, the majority of their tattoos now concealed.

West, noticing the three making their way toward them, slaps Rowan in the chest—indicating that he needs to see what West is seeing. Eve's cheeks flush as the males' gazes tell her everything. Luca's eyes are hungry as he watches her approach.

Rowan, on the other hand, puts two fingers in his mouth and whistles. Breaking away from his brothers, he jogs over, and throws an arm around Eve.

"Damn, girl! We need to get you out more often! Eve's riding with me!"

Playfully tugging her toward the vehicle in front, she briefly picks out Luca with a slight scowl on his face. A little jealousy never hurts anyone.

Eve reminds herself to thank Beth for everything.

Slight chaos ensues as more people pour out in their finest attire. Grimacing, Eve spots Lucia and Sophia in the mix. She isn't sure if what they are wearing would be considered clothing. Sequined bathing suit tops and miniskirts paired with go-go boots. Eve can't help but watch from the front seat passenger mirror as they approach Luca, climbing into a separate Humvee with him.

"What's wrong? You don't like a little Latin flavor?" Rowan jokes. Eve's reaction to Lucia and Sophia's arrival must have been obvious.

"No, she just doesn't like attention-seeking robots," Maggie snaps. Cuddled up with West in the middle row, Eve spots Martin in the back, awkwardly trying to create some distance from their PDA.

"I like you, Maggie." Rowan laughs, genuine.

"Same dude. Same."

West plants a small kiss on Maggie's neck, in obvious awe of the creature beside him.

They're just about to pull out, when Riley, of all people, marches across the gravel. Rowan lowers Eve's window.

"Good evening, sir. Care to join?" Rowan asks politely.

"Thank you, but no. You guys know the rules. Be back by three a.m., no later, and stick close to Martin. He's still on duty and will make you aware of any impending threat."

"Thank you for your sacrifice, buddy. I know how much you were dying to get your dance on…." Rowan winks at Martin in the rearview mirror, who only shakes his head.

Riley nods, a cue for them to be off, as the cars start to move. Ripping down the driveway and out the gates, they trade dirt for pavement, heading north on the freeway.

West and Maggie are whispering and laughing as Rowan lowers the radio, wanting to engage with Eve.

"Why did you have to cover up? I was excited to see Martin's work!" he says, indicating her tattoos.

"Beth and Maggie forced me into this one. Not my idea."

Eve squirms, uncomfortable, as the slit in her dress keeps shifting, exposing more skin. And her itching arms are driving her mad. It takes all her willpower not to scratch the already-raw skin being harassed by the tight fabric.

"You look amazing." Rowan is almost bashful as he gives her a sweet smile, which she returns. He's wearing a powder blue collared shirt that hugs his toned physique, and Eve isn't minding it one bit. Rowan keeps glancing at her exposed leg and back to her face, but it doesn't bother her. Eve doesn't feel like she is being objectified, just admired.

And she finds herself not minding Rowan's attention as much as she did before.

They all chat, the mood light, for what has to be an hour before they arrive at the outskirts of a city. The twinkling lights from the multiple houses and businesses sprinkle the valley before them.

"We...are somewhere in New Mexico, I think? Doesn't matter, as long as there is a club with alcohol, and guess what—we have located a club with alcohol!"

West corrects him, "Martin located a club with alcohol! What my brother is trying to say is that there is a club, and you're probably going to see more than one tipsy Zapper tonight."

"But what if there's an attack? Don't you guys have to be ready at all times?" Eve ponders.

"There's a pill for that—instantly sobers, but it leaves you with a sour stomach for days. And there are only fifteen of us out tonight of the forty, give or take, currently in residence at Evergreen. I think we're allowed to let loose a little."

Rowan cups her chin with his right hand, the left still steering, and then focuses back on the road. Driving through the city, Eve soaks everything in. Laundromats, gas stations...normal people living their normal lives. When you're pulled away from society for an extended period of time, you really appreciate the little things. Especially with her new eyes, she quite literally could see everything more clearly.

The city starts to shift from smaller businesses to taller corporate structures, indicating that they are downtown. Rounding a corner, a rectangular building with neon blue and pink siding reads "The Velvet Lounge."

Trusting the Humvees to excited teenage valets, the striking group heads toward the front entrance of the club, bypassing a significant line wrapping around the building. Sparing a glance behind her, Eve is disappointed to see Luca walking next to Sophia. She's touching her hair and laughing, while Luca is telling her some humorous story.

Rowan sweetly slips his large paw into hers and starts swinging their arms back and forth like schoolchildren, dragging her attention back to him.

"Any guy that's looking at anyone but you right now is an idiot."

Eve's jaw drops slightly, unaware that her surveillance has been that obvious.

"Do you even mean half the things that come out of your mouth?" Eve snorts.

"Stick with me and find out...."

Rowan squeezes her hand and smiles as they pay off the bouncer, letting their entire group cut the line.

"And now, we dance!" Rowan yells over the house music, guiding Eve onto the crowded dance floor. She covers her face in her hands, mortified. Eve was prepared to sit at a table all night and watch everyone else grinding and gyrating, but she hadn't planned for this.

Removing her hands from her eyes, she tries to bolt—but Rowan grabs her waist, bringing her to lean her back against him. Entranced by the music, the energy, and the smell of his aftershave, she slowly starts to let go. Eve decides to take Rowan's advice and focus on what is right in front of her.

Which just happens to be him.

Chapter 29

Eve gets lost with Rowan as they dance. Her feet are starting to hurt, but no less than her already-throbbing arms. She honestly doesn't care. Laughing more than probably one should, she's never had this much fun in her adult life thus far.

The DJ switches to a slow song as Eve rests her head against Rowan's chest engulfed in his embrace as they shuffle from side to side.

"You're all sweaty," Rowan teases.

"So are you, but I currently don't care."

"Are you glad you came out tonight?" Rowan whispers in her ear, sending a pleasant chill down her spine.

"Actually, yes. I needed this."

"So needy...."

"Speaking of 'needy,' I need to run to the ladies' room. Any ideas of where that may be?"

Rowan points to the right of the bar and squeezes her hand as they navigate through the couples. Splitting apart, Rowan heads over to the bar to buy them some drinks and join the ever-moody Tate, who hasn't left his stool all evening.

Making her way through the crowd, she winces, aware of two thick blisters, one on each heel. Eve wonders if they have a first aid kit in this place, or maybe Martin has something in one of his kits he could dole out.

Thankfully, there's no queue as she locates the ladies' restroom. Entering a stall, she hears the doors open and two more familiar voices.

"Ugh, I hate her! She has literally been all over Rowan since we arrived."

Eve recognizes that voice—Lucia.

"He's talking to Tate right now, and she has disappeared somewhere. If you want him, go make a move. You know how Rowan likes his charity cases...."

Normally, Eve would have kept sitting in that stall until they had completed their childish gossiping, but not tonight.

Flushing loudly for effect, she throws the stall door open and steps out.

Sophia and Lucia are reapplying lip gloss in the mirror, and Sophia's gets slightly smudged as she whips to face Eve.

"Look, I know both of you don't like me. And it's pretty obvious that I don't like you either, but let's set a few things straight. It's okay that you both see Maggie and I as a threat. Which you should, because we are catching up and excelling at everything that's thrown our way. We are right on your heels, and you know it. When it comes to the Quinns, you also see us as competition. Which you also should. Word of advice? If you want to nail down Rowan or anyone else, I suggest playing a little hard to get? The way both of you throw yourselves at any guy that walks past is a tad bit desperate."

Sophia growls, lunging at Eve, but Lucia grabs her around her middle, holding her back. Eve notices a silver moonstone ring on Lucia's left ring finger as her knuckles whiten in an effort to detain her sister. Unperturbed, Eve steps around them, washes her hands, casually using a soft towel to blot them dry. Sophia is still trying to get to her.

"Let go of me! Lucia! Let go!"

"No, if you attack her, we'll be in serious trouble!" Lucia whines.

"Night, ladies."

Eve struts past them and back out into the bar, and a smug smile tugs at her lips. Scanning the crowd for Rowan, she notices his distinct braids at the bar, and is about to join him when a large hand grabs hers.

Immediately on the offense, she is ready to attack when she realizes the man holding her hand is Luca.

Wasting no time, he tugs, dragging her toward a set of private rooms behind them. Entering a hallway, Eve looks in each as they pass—but they're empty. More than likely reserved for VIPs, or the early morning hours when dancing is done but drinking is not.

Identical, each is set up with a round table and padded booths adorned with beaded curtains. Mirrors are on all sides, the lighting a low pink with a glass table in the middle. Luca doesn't stop until they reach the very last one, and moving the beads aside, he brings her in.

"Luca, what are you doing….?"

Eve sighs. The music is lower back here, and she can speak without yelling. He still holds her right hand, his thumb tracing circles on the back.

Torn, Eve is so incredibly torn. Wanting to go back to Rowan, but needing to be next to Luca, she simply waits to see what happens next.

"Were you trying to make me jealous? Because it sure as hell worked."

Luca steps closer to her, and her mouth goes dry.

"No, what?! You were with Sophia. I was just enjoying myself."

He steps even closer.

"How many times do I have to tell you that I am not into Sophia? Our parents were friends. I've known her most of my life and I care about her, but not in the way that you think."

Luca is right in front of her. His breath smells of mint as he leans down toward her.

"You are so beautiful…."

Eve takes a step back, putting a bit of distance between them.

"I don't think we should do this," Eve whispers, trying to convince herself as well.

Luca steps forward, closing the gap once more.

"I have wanted to do this since I first saw you in Seattle. The first day we were on assignment. You had taken Maggie for ice cream, and the two of you were sitting on a bench by the waterfront. You just sat there, holding the melting cone, the wind tossing your hair and your eyes on the Ferris wheel. I could tell that you were hurting, but you were doing it for Maggie. That is who you are, Eve. The kind of person who puts everyone else first. Eve, I see you."

And that is the last thing he utters before she kisses him.

Fighting isn't the only thing Luca is good at, as he teases her, biting her lower lip. His fingers run down her spine, giving her goosebumps as they end up on the couch. Luca is grabbing her right shoulder, softly kissing her neck, when Eve screams in pain.

Leaping from the couch, hands in the air and eyes wide, he says hoarsely, "What's wrong? What did I do?!"

Eve is hunched over in agony, holding her shoulder.

"Nothing. You...didn't do anything. My arms."

Eve's eyes are tearing, a pain response, and a cold sweat has soaked her bangs. She rocks back and forth in anguish.

Luca rushes forward, kneeling in front of her. Moving her bangs off her forehead, her cups her face. Tilting her head back, her pupils are blown.

"Shit, stay here, don't move." Running from the booth, he is back within minutes. Three Quinns—Luca, Martin, and Tate—break into the room and hurry to help.

Opening a black case, Martin throws on surgical gloves and retrieves a pair of small scissors. "I am going to cut your dress at the sleeves. I need to see what is going on."

Eve only nods, her teeth chattering. Martin deftly slits each one past the shoulder, and hears fibers ripping as he pulls them away to expose her inflamed skin.

"Tate, get the Humvee! Now!" Martin barks. Tate doesn't hesitate, sprinting from the room.

"Eve, you are having an allergic reaction. We need to remove the solar cells," Martin explains calmly, checking her pulse.

"What? No... No!" She starts to crumble.

Luca sweeps her up in his arms, rushing her from the room and screaming at anyone in his way to move. Eve spots Maggie dancing with West, but her sister freezes, the blood draining from her face. She sprints over, an impressive feat in her tall heels, worry riddling her exquisite features.

"Eve? Are you okay? What is going on?!" She hears Maggie's voice cracking somewhere behind her.

The pain is unbearable. Biting her lip to keep from crying out, Eve tastes blood. Tate grabs the keys from the valet and hops into the driver's side. The car roars to life. Luca gently sets her on her feet, and Rowan is there, holding her up.

"West, get Maggie into the second car. We need to move."

The lovebirds do not hesitate, grabbing another set of keys from the valet and hurrying to the second Hummer.

Seeing her gentle friends' faces, she can no longer hold back her tears. Rowan makes soothing noises, running his palms up and down her cold exposed back.

"They have to take them out, Rowan...."

Her arms are not the only thing hurting.

"We'll fix it, okay? Martin will fix it. He always does...."

Luca steps up into the backseat and turns, holding out his hand to Eve. She takes it as he helps her in. Opening the back end, Martin grabs more cases and then slams it shut, joining Eve and Luca.

Rowan barely makes it into the front passenger side before Tate floors it. Peeling out of the parking lot, they fly onto the main road. Ignoring traffic lights, stop signs, and the basic rules of driving.

"How far are we from Evergreen?" Luca barks.

Checking the map on the screen built into the dash, Tate quickly says, "Hour and a half, give or take."

"We need to be there in forty-five...." Hearing the urgency in Martin's words, Tate floors it.

Eve's throat is starting to swell. Her breathing is laborious, wheezing in and out of her constricting vocal cords. Opening a kit on his lap, Martin locates a syringe, turns quickly, wiping Eve's exposed leg, and stabs her in the thigh.

She screams once more, but it comes out more as a strained gurgle. And then her body begins to relax. Her eyelids feel so heavy as they start to close, and the last thing she sees is Luca as he whispers, "Sleep."

And then nothing.

Chapter 30

Beep. Beep. Beep.

Eve's eyes are still shut, but she hears the sounds of machines beside her.

Groggily, she stirs, the ceiling lights in the room blinding her sensitive eyes.

A chair grates as someone gets up beside her, standing.

"Eve? It's Maggie...."

Hearing her sister's voice, she looks over. The petite redhead has a blanket wrapped around her, but the straps from her borrowed orange dress peek through. Her mascara is smeared, and from her swollen eyes, Eve can tell she's been crying.

"You scared me, you idiot."

Seeing her trying to sit up, Maggie grabs a remote control, adjusting the bed's back until Eve nods that she is comfortable.

"What happened after Martin drugged me?"

Her voice is gravelly, vocal cords strained from her ordeal.

"Martin had to remove the battery strips in your tattoos. For some reason, your body rejected them. He said it's never happened before."

No surprise there. Martin had already told her in the club that they had to be removed, but she had reserved a shred of hope that maybe, if they had gotten to Evergreen in time, that something else could have been done.

Life wins again. Eve Abbott is once again a failure.

"Okay," she mumbles numbly.

"But, hey! He's already started working on it. Martin said he'll figure it out and that he'll try again. For now, you just get really cool scars."

Both her limbs are heavily bandaged, but when Eve applies light pressure with her fingertips, there is little to no pain.

"Martin said you can leave whenever you're ready. Might be better to be back in our room?"

Eve knows that Maggie is trying, but she just wants to be alone.

"Can you give me a few minutes? I'll get changed, and then we can go."

Swinging her bare legs to the floor, Eve turns her back to Maggie. She hears her exit as Eve reaches for her temples, light-headed.

How could one of the best nights of her life turn into one of the worst? What must everyone think of her now?

Feeling an impending headache, she gingerly stands, retrieving a stack of clean clothing from a table beside her. She pulls on sweatpants, and then, carefully, a soft t-shirt over her head. Lastly, sliding her feet into a pair of flip-flops. Pink, with hearts—they have to belong to Beth.

Exiting the room, Eve recognizes the tunnel. Evergreen has a secret hospital as well near the laboratory? Trickily concealed by another fake wall, its existence makes sense with how dangerous their jobs are.

Or were. For Eve, this might be the end of the road.

Shuffling around a corner, she grimaces upon seeing who has gathered.

West, Luca, Rowan, and Martin are there, as well as Riley. All the Quinns are still in their clubbing clothes, dark circles marring their tired faces. Riley steps forward in his usual uniform, as Eve mentally begs him not to give a speech.

"We…all had a bit of a scare last night. Your body's rejection of the procedure is, I'm sure, disappointing. But we will get to the root of it."

Staring at her toes, she starts to walk…and keeps walking, her head down. Eve hears her name being called. It might have been Luca or Rowan, but she doesn't stop to find out. Making her way up the three flight of stairs to their room, she keeps walking all the way into the bathroom and turns the lock.

Turning on the tub, she sits on the edge, lowering her pounding head into her hands. Several minutes pass, and if Maggie has seen her and followed, she thankfully doesn't knock.

The mirrors in the bathroom start to fog as Eve rises, discarding her clothing. Standing naked, she removes the bandages as well—first her left, then the right. Using a towel, Eve wipes the steam from the mirror, giving her a clearer view of the damage done.

The black lines are gone, replaced with light pink, puckered scars. Still in the same shapes and patterns…they tease her. Broadcasting her unworthiness. They're hideous, but they don't hurt. Even as she lowers herself into the scalding bathtub, her raw flesh only stings slightly.

The water turns cold, but Eve doesn't move.

"Hey, you still in there?"

Startled by Maggie's worried voice, Eve causes a small tidal wave of water to cascade to the tile.

It takes a moment before she responds with a hoarse, "Yes."

"Do you need anything?"

"No."

Eve hears her walk away, and she shakily dries and dresses, finding Maggie sitting on her bed.

"Can I see?" Maggie inquires, direct as always.

"They're scars, Maggie...."

"And I want to see them!"

"They're not yours to see! Back off!" she croaks.

Angrily, Eve storms toward the door, stopping mid-stride when she realizes she has nowhere to go. Nowhere she can be alone on this camera-infested property.

"Just show them to me. Get it over with, rip off the Band-Aid!" Maggie demands, getting right in her face.

"Maggie...." Eve's raw voice cracks as angry tears spring to her eyes.

"Take off your goddamn shirt, but leave your bra on. I don't want to see 'that'...." Maggie has tears in her eyes as well as she snickers at her own joke. But she means it.

Too weak to fight her, Eve does as she is told, tossing her long-sleeved shirt onto her plaid comforter.

Eve is crying in earnest as Maggie studies her newly formed fibrous tissue.

"Good. Now, never cover up again. Anyone that has a problem with you, shut them up. You don't need their batteries, Eve. You're a bad bitch all on your own, and you will not let this, or anyone, stop you."

Wiping the tears from her eyes, Eve can't help but giggle.

"Was that supposed to be a pep talk?"

"Yup."

"It was pretty good," Eve states, impressed.

"I know. Now hug me, because I need to get the hell out of this dress."

Laughing, Eve squeezes her baby sister tightly. Then a relieved Maggie escapes for her turn in the bathroom as Eve crawls into her inviting sheets.

How she misses her books in this moment. It would be glorious to read without needing the assistance of her glasses. Her vision correction had nothing to do with her allergic reaction to the solar cells, and her body seems to be handling that change perfectly.

Unsure of what to do next, Eve starts to count the boards in the ceiling when she hears a quiet knock.

The door opens, and a freshly showered Luca enters, back in their standardized garb.

"Hey," he says, awkwardly, shoving his hands in his pockets.

Swinging her feet back to the floor, she gets up and walks over to him.

"Aren't you supposed to be in the cave?" Eve asks.

"Yes."

"And yet, you are here."

"I am."

"Aren't you going to get in trouble?"

"Probably not."

"What do you want?"

Luca steps closer, so close that their toes are almost touching. With one hand, he tilts her chin up, forcing her to look at him.

"You. I want you."

Eve goes to shake her head, but both of his hands stop her dismissal. And then he kisses her. Tenderly, and soft, before enveloping her into a careful hug.

"Gross, take this somewhere else!" Maggie exclaims, pretending to barf. Towel wrapped around her, she digs through the oak dresser for her underwear.

Smirking, Luca nudges Eve, and asks, "Do you want to see my room?"

"Yes, she does! Bye!" Maggie answers for her, still not able to find whatever she is looking for in the drawer.

"As long as you have somewhere to sit." Eve's response is joking, but serious. Putting his arm around her, he patiently helps her down the stairs to the second floor, leading her to the first door to the left of the landing with an eagle carved upon it.

Luca's room is nothing like Beth's or Eve and Maggie's. The layout is the same, but the walls have been painted dark blue. No four-poster or canopy bed, just a mattress and box spring on the floor in the center of the space. On his dresser is a record player, and covering the floor is crate after crate of records. The only messy part about his room is the actual bed, the rest seems to be well organized.

"You promised me a place to sit," Eve teases hoarsely, her complexion turning gray from fatigue.

Luca takes her hand and leads her over to rumpled comforter and pillows.

"Best seat in the house," Luca flirts as Eve plops down.

Walking away from Eve, he seems to be looking for something among his records. It only takes him a minute before he pulls out a disc, placing it onto a turntable. The music that it starts to emit is unfamiliar.

"This is nice…." Eve finds herself laying down, tucking one of his soft down pillows under her throbbing head.

"Nice? This is more than nice—this is Miles Davis."

"Who?" Eve mumbles, half awake.

"I will pretend you didn't say that…."

Luca heads back over to her and crouches down.

"Do you need anything? Water?"

Eve's eyes have closed, but she is still awake and listening.

"Water would be nice."

Eve opens her crystal-blue eyes and looks at Luca. He takes in her pale skin and pink lips. Her thick eyebrows partially obscured by her fringe.

Luca has never wanted to protect someone more in his life than he wants to protect her. What a fool he has been. A total jerk, really. This stunning, resilient woman didn't deserve his rejection or aloofness.

He had his reasons, and tried to get her out of his mind, but it was impossible. Luca has run out of excuses for why they shouldn't be together. She doesn't even know how incredible she is, and it just makes him want her even more.

Luca is in love with her.

And he knows that being in love with an Abbott will prove costly.

For now, Eve will stay in the dark. She will not find out the one thing they are still holding back. Because if Eve ever discovers what her parents did to his...

It would ruin everything.

Chapter 31

I am in a car, in the station wagon.

My hair has been cut short—right below my chin, eliminating the matted evidence.

In my time in the white room, my eyesight has begun to deteriorate.

Thick, new glasses sit on the bridge of my nose, unwelcome but necessary.

A man adjusts the rearview mirror until I notice him looking at me in the back seat.

"How you doing, kiddo?" asks Orion. My father.

I will not speak. What they have done to me is unforgivable.

"Leave her alone. She will adjust." Adel fixes her bun with her delicate hands, her red nail polish unmarred.

How dare my mother be so relaxed.

How fake she is, coming to my defense now.

Those nails.

I saw them injecting me over and over again with thick needles. I saw those nails dragging me from the white room.

I saw those nails covering my screams as they drilled into my bones.

I saw those red nails securing my shackles in the glass tank.

I hate those long, crimson-painted fingers.

My mother turns toward me. Love and concern in her eyes, as she reaches back to pat my knee.

I flinch.

"It is okay, Eve. You will forget all of this. Trust me. It will be nothing but a bad dream...."

Eve sits straight up, disoriented. It's nighttime and the moon peeks through the window, illuminating crates on the floor. Despite the cold temperature, her body is covered in sweat. A hand touches her leg, and she recoils.

Luca, it is only Luca.

Shirtless, he's lying on his stomach, but he is wide awake.

Eve wants to forget. She wants to forget everything.

She kisses him. Turning so that he is on his back, she climbs on top, straddling his waist, and his powerful hands grab her hips. Breaking the kiss, he helps remove her thermal. She's about to take off her sports bra as well, but then she notices them.

Her new scars.

Looking down, she sees the pink, thin, raised lines covering both of her limbs and freezes.

"Eve, it's okay." Luca rises to his forearms, his forehead creasing.

She slides off of his lap.

"It's okay. Martin always figures things out. I bet, in less than a week, they'll be put back."

She doesn't speak, just nods.

Goosebumps cover her skin as Luca starts to gently rub her shoulders.

"Come over here, you're cold."

Pulling her under the comforter, he hugs her to his chest. Luca's arms radiate heat as Eve decides to open up.

"But...what if he doesn't?"

"Who, Martin? He will...."

Hugging her tighter, Eve feels her eyes closing once more.

"He will."

If Luca believes, then she will too. Together, they fall back under sleep's spell.

When Eve wakes again at five in the morning without an alarm, she groans. Her body doesn't seem to realize that today, she will be able to sleep in. Riley has given her one day, and then she will be required back in the cave.

She's in Luca's room, but the spot beside her is empty. Locating her top within one of his boxes of records, she slides it on and lays back down. Hearing footsteps, Luca exits his closet having come from the bathroom.

Noticing her awake, he smiles, having already dressed for the day in his training gear.

"Nice hair," he taunts, pointing out what must be her bed head.

"I styled it just for you," Eve retorts, causing Luca to laugh.

Luca, *laughing*, now that is something new. It softens him. And Eve finds herself laughing with him. Leaning down, he gives her a passionate kiss on the mouth and quickly backs away.

"You hungry?"

She can tell that he is. A guy his size doesn't maintain his physique by dieting. Eve had missed at least three meals in the past twenty-four hours, but she only feels the dull thud of hunger.

"I could eat," Eve decides, swinging her bare feet to the floor.

"Do you want to go shower, and meet me at the dining hall?" Luca is almost shy as he asks, which is even more endearing.

"Are you sure you want to be seen with me?"

"Actually, yes."

They share a few more kisses and then part. For some reason, she thinks of Rowan. How will it affect him, seeing Luca and her—together? Will he still want to hang out? Eve doesn't think she could take it if she lost him too.

If she's honest with herself, Eve isn't even sure how she feels about Luca and her dating. He only recently has shown her kindness. Events in her life seem to keep happening at a rapid-fire pace and she is finding it hard, mentally, to catch up. Luca is still very much a stranger, and beyond physical attraction, she doesn't really know that much about him.

But what she does know sets her soul on fire.

Leaving his room, she turns to find Maggie on the stairwell.

"Well, good morning to you!" Maggie purrs.

"Not now…" Eve flushes, making her way to the stairs.

"What? We're all adults. Doing adult things. With *very attractive* adults…."

Maggie is enjoying this.

Rolling her eyes, Eve states, "I'm going to go shower," as she heads toward the third floor.

"Alone, or…?"

Eve cuts her off before she can finish her sentence.

"I'll be down in ten."

"Uh-huh…."

Half an hour later, as she walks into the kitchen freshly bathed, the sizzling potatoes on a large skillet cause Eve's mouth to water. Grabbing a plate, she piles on buttermilk biscuits, gravy, and sausage. Turning toward the table, she's surprised to see a full house. Maggie and West are side by side, already finished but chatting, and across the table is Luca. He's saved her a seat and eating like his life depends on it. Even while stuffing his face, he's adorable.

Setting down her plate, she receives overly friendly "hellos" and head nods. Everyone is trying to act normal but failing. Riley or Maggie has obviously given everyone the "don't treat her any differently" spiel. Losing her appetite, Eve pushes the potatoes and eggs around her plate with her limp fork.

Feeling a hand on her neck, she looks over as Luca wipes his delicious-looking mouth with a napkin. The touch makes it plain to everyone at breakfast that he is staking his claim.

Riley seems unsurprised. He's aware of all that goes on at Evergreen and has probably already read a report that Eve Abbott had spent the night in Luca Quinn's room. Fraternization isn't against the rules as long as it doesn't get in the way. A small gift to these soldiers, especially when most risked their lives on a daily basis.

Eve looks next to Tate, who shrugs, but continues with his breakfast burrito. Silently giving his approval.

But not everyone is on board.

Sophia's intense gaze is molten lava, and Eve can tell that she's ready to erupt at any moment. Their little chat in the ladies' bathroom probably didn't help. Lucia, grabbing seconds from the cook, doesn't seem to share her sister's indignation. Having her sights set on Rowan, Luca and his love life don't matter to her.

Rowan. Scanning the room, he isn't here. But neither is Beth. Both must be already hard at work.

Once breakfast is complete, the warriors make their way to the cave, dividing up into conditioning, hand-to-hand combat,

and weapons. Eve is allowed to join in Maggie's weapons training, but only on an observation level.

Today will be Maggie's first day working with Rowan with
her new solar cells, and even though technically Eve has the day
off, she doesn't want to miss it. She's relieved when she spots
him, whirring a long spear as the Abbott sisters jog to the back
area of the mats. Spotting them, Rowan sets his spear back in the
stand, and engulfs them both in a big hug.

Eve has never been more relieved.

Maggie goes to stretch, giving Rowan a chance to speak to
Eve somewhat privately.

"Hey kid, you hanging in there?"

She nods, her smile somewhat strained.

"Cheer up, Martin will—"

Eve cuts him off.

"I know, Martin will come up with something."

"At least you have Luca to keep you busy in the meantime."
Rowan tries to pass his words off as a joke, but she can tell he
is hurt.

She stutters, "Oh—I, um…" and is about to blurt an apology
when Rowan pulls Eve into another warm hug.

"I was joking. Relax. I will take you however I can get you."

Torn. Eve officially feels herself romantically torn between
Luca and Rowan. The two Quinn brothers couldn't be more
different—Rowan, so sweet and solid, his personality never
wavering. And then Luca—passionate, wild, and exciting, but
unpredictable.

Eve already made her choice the moment she kissed Luca
in that club. No one forced her to do so, especially not while
Rowan was waiting for her at the bar. Rowan may be right for
her in different ways, but for right now, she's made her decision.

And with a sigh, they join Maggie to stretch on the floor.

Watching Maggie interact with Rowan the next couple of hours is pure torture. They run through a few different weapons before settling on the spear that Rowan was wielding earlier. As the munitions expert, he'd already anticipated what might best suit her.

"Do you remember the ax you were carrying, when the level one attacked back in Saintsville?"

Slightly breathless, Rowan is taking Maggie through the ropes, holding a spear of his own.

Per Rowan's instruction, they are sparring at 10 percent power. Both sets of tattoos are a dark velvet red.

"Ha. Yeah. Why?" Maggie inquires, thrusting the sharp tip toward his skull, which he deflects.

"I knew then that you just needed something hard that you could hit people with!"

Maggie and Rowan start laughing. *Crack, crack, crack*, the noise of their spears colliding echoes off the walls.

Taking a short break, Maggie skips over to Eve and kneels down beside her, grabbing her water bottle and drinking.

"This totally sucks, huh?" Maggie mutters, wiping her face with a towel.

Rowan joins them, his own water bottle in hand. Squatting before them, he slaps Eve's extended legs playfully.

"I'm sorry. You can still learn a lot, even from just watching."

Eve sighs, and nods.

"And speaking of watching, we have an extra special treat for you guys later."

Both sisters perk up.

"What kind of treat?" Eve asks, curious.

"You'll see...."

Rowan waggles his eyebrows, his enthusiasm barely contained. Whatever the surprise is, it must be good.

Chapter 32

A fter dinner, they're issued tactical gear from the armory. Turns out, the armory is one of the "off limits" buildings across from the main house that the girls have never been in before.

For Eve, this just involves a paper-thin vest that, according to Martin, is ten times stronger than Kevlar. With the vest and her usual uniform, she is good to go.

Maggie is issued a vest as well, which can only mean one thing.

They are going on their first ride-along.

Eve, technically, should be resting, but she is thankful that Riley didn't take this moment away from her. This mission was no doubt planned days before her body's rejection of her implants.

Various Zappers—some they know, some unfamiliar—roam around the organized warehouse, packing their artillery of choice.

After months upon months of training, the Abbotts are being thrust into a real-life situation. From the safety of the car, for now, but it's a start.

Riley thought it best to begin with something easy. They'd discovered a nest via satellite. Three or four smokers, level ones, camped out near a power plant fifty miles away. Apparently, this is a common occurrence. The mutations find the electrical potency irresistible. Their siphoning is a dead giveaway, causing power outages, which the local government then has to cover up, blaming their citizens' overuse of air conditioning or the unpredictability of the weather.

More of a nuisance than a real threat, the Zappers have orders to exterminate.

Close to six, the sun is setting as Eve and Maggie follow their assigned team to the driveway. Thick cases are being loaded into the Humvees as they divide into separate cars.

Beth's locks are dyed temporarily pink and rolled into a tight bun on the top of her head. She's helping Martin pack up the last vehicle, while Tate and Rowan slide various weapons from a rolling cart into custom-built cubbies.

Amongst the small crowd, Eve also spots West, Luca, and unfortunately, Sophia. She is planted firmly in front of Luca, telling him some story about her falling in a hole on their last mutant hunting endeavor and spraining her ankle. His arms are crossed as he listens, but he is polite nonetheless.

Seeing Eve, Luca excuses himself and walks straight toward her.

"Hi," he utters, a sexy grin parting his lips, before he places those very lips on hers.

Shocked by a second public display of affection, she finally relaxes, but the sound of whistling and clapping causes them to break apart.

The culprits of the heckling are Beth and Tate, the latter of which has been warming up to Eve of late. Long gone are Tate's death stares and demeaning comments. She and Maggie have somehow earned his respect, and they are no longer his least favorite people on the planet.

Spotting Rowan, Eve's heart feels a pang.

He smiles at her, but his eyes are strained.

Luca whispers in her ear, "This is going to be fun," before planting one more quick kiss and motioning for them to get in their respective vehicles.

Assuming they are with Luca, Eve and Maggie climb in first, followed by Sophia and Tate.

The cars start, and they are off.

For their sake, Luca starts to explain the plan, the other Zappers having already been briefed.

They would install a light row—like the one they used back in Saintsville but on a smaller scale—and draw the smokers to them. After they had been blasted, the mutations would be in a weakened state. Then, Luca and the rest would work in pairs to finish them off.

An hour into their drive, the sun had set, leaving them to their task in the darkness. Heading through town and turning off on a rural road near the outskirts, it reminds Eve of the way to their grandmother's home in Saintsville. Another dirt road, another lake, but this time, they are aware of the danger ahead.

Reaching a tall metal fence with intense barbwire lining the top, the cars halt in front of a gate. Beth hops out of the last car and strolls up to a hanging box mounted on the side. Lifting the lid, she types in a code, inserts a key, and turns.

The gate slides open.

Jogging back, Beth climbs into her Humvee and again they're off, stirring up copious amounts of dirt on the bumpy road.

"Martin, let me know when," Luca orders through their cars' linked intercom. A map is pulled up on a large screen, and Eve can see their three green dots coming closer to one main red circle.

"Another minute. There's a plateau to the right of the generators," Martin responds.

Eve feels the frenetic energy. The anticipation of the other hunters. Oddly, she swears that she also feels the power radiating from the industrial buildings that are slowly coming into view.

"Now!" Martin barks, and Luca slams on his brakes. The moment the cars are in park, everyone but Eve and Maggie swarms out, quickly getting to work. Beth and Tate are carrying cases and dropping them ten feet apart. They repeat this until eight are visible on the rubble.

Martin has his tablet in hand, more than likely tracking the movement of the smokers. Making sure they don't intercept the Zappers before they are ready.

Enthralled, Maggie and Eve watch while Sophia and Tate open each case and remove four-foot-long light panels, with a rototiller-type base attached on the bottom. One at a time, when the lights are lined up, they press a button and the rototiller spins, digging until the panel is firmly ingrained in the dirt.

After all eight are in place, Martin taps his tablet, and the panels rise into the air, turning to face the direction of the power plant generators.

A quick test, a tiny flash, and a thumbs-up from Martin.

"I want to be out there!" Maggie pouts, spotting West assembling a nasty-looking gun. Eve can tell Maggie's also concerned. Her little sister knows that West does this sort of thing all the time, but it's one thing to hear about it from him, and another to have a front-row seat.

"I would be no use out there. But you're kind of terrifying with that spear…."

"I know, right?!" Maggie agrees. "It's a shame."

The Zappers are ready to move in.

Heading stealthily away from the Humvees, Luca is in the lead. He starts to jog, and the others closely follow, fanning out. Only Martin stays behind, as he unhurriedly walks over to Eve and Maggie.

Throwing open the driver's side, he enters a code into the keypad, and the map switches to a live view from Luca's body-cam. Eve and Maggie lean forward in unison, neither of them breathing as they see his unit slowing to a walk, and then to a stop.

"Thought you might want to watch," Martin states as he climbs back down, shuts the door, and moves to stand near the light panels.

Luca makes some sort of hand signal, and Rowan fires off a blazing arrow into a dark space between two buildings. It embeds in the tin siding, and unearthly shrieks ring out in response.

"Oh, this is not good."

Maggie grabs Eve's leg, squeezing hard. Luca motions, and Rowan fires one more arrow, this time directly into a utility pole above. The sky is briefly illuminated as they see two dark masses attached to the cables. *Flash*. The smokers drop to the ground. *Flash*. They charge directly at the waiting Zappers.

"Run! Oh my god, run!" Eve shrieks. She feels the thrum of power surrounding her as her skin starts to heat. The interior of the car seems to be closing in. Eve feels like she is suffocating, but she can't look away.

And run they do. Luca, stopping to let the others pass, swiftly pulls up his rifle and fires off several rounds, striking a level one in the front. Now, five smokers in total—the three in back that were starting to lose interest shriek at Luca in anger, joining their fellow mutations in their chase.

"Get out of there!" Eve bellows, slapping the front seat in agitation, perspiration pooling on her skin and soaking her bangs.

"Eve…are you okay?" Maggie asks, alarmed by Eve's current state. Even more so than her "kind of, but not official" boyfriend currently running for his life.

She doesn't respond as Luca and the rest round the corner. The sisters no longer need to watch the screen to see what's happening. The Zappers are full-out sprinting, occasionally firing a gun, shooting an arrow, further angering the already-enraged monsters. Their fog-like tentacles dart out, attempting to grab their prey, until one catches Beth around the ankle and pulls.

Eve and Maggie gasp in horror as Beth flies backwards, being engulfed by one of the monsters.

"Martin, now!" Luca roars, and Eve and Maggie duck, shielding their eyes. They count to five, per their training, and look back to their comrades, needing to see how this ends.

Chaos. All hell has broken loose.

They see Beth still alive, but her skin is covered in burns. Her red tattoos gleam as she flings a kind of rope with a hook on the end, wrapping it several times around the mutant that had attacked her, rendering it immobile. Pulling hard, the rope flashes and the smoker screams, while Tate moves in with his saws and finishes it.

At the same time, Sophia and another Zapper dart in and out, inflicting several cuts with their flaming blades, taking out another smoker.

With his rifle, Luca must have taken out another—but the sisters missed it, only spotting him running away from a smoking pile of ash.

Three down, and two to go.

And the last two are no match for West. Eve hadn't previously seen the weapon strapped to his back, with a sort of hose attached to his right arm. The nozzle extends well beyond his hand, and electrified flames rip outwards, lighting the two level ones on fire.

From there, kills are quick. More bullets, knives, and Beth's wicked rope.

Finally over, Eve is shaking and drenched. Her heart feels like it might burst, and her breathing is rapid and shallow. Maggie can't stop looking between the field and her sister, unsure if she should call for help or congratulate the victors.

Relaxing, the Zappers gather in a rough circle and then break apart to repack their gear.

But something is wrong.

Martin starts to cuss, which he never does, and yells, "Trap! This is a trap! Get ready!"

Lightning starts to strike, lighting up the sky.

Looking out the window, Eve sees a swarming mass of what looks like birds, but as it approaches—fliers. Hundreds upon hundreds, they light up the sky and are headed directly toward them.

There is no time to run.

Maggie unbuckles her seat belt and hops from the car. Running to the second Humvee, she grabs her spear from the rear and sprints until she is next to West.

Their enemy isn't only in the sky, but also coming from the ground as another swarm of jumpers and rollers barrels from around the power plant.

They are all going to die.

Eve feels every single one. She knows the mutants' numbers without counting and their power without testing them. The irises in her eyes drain of color, replaced with solid black as her hair starts to rise in the air. She doesn't remember leaving the car as she walks toward them.

Smoke and sparks trickle, and then flow from Eve's hands. They start to spin, round and round, until Eve is in the center of an electrified tornado of her own making. Up and up, at least five hundred feet in the air it spins, with Eve serenely in the center.

Then it starts to move.

Eve is unharmed as it passes over and through her, ripping apart everything in its path.

"Move," Eve whispers, but the whisper carries, and the Zappers scatter.

Only then does she really let go.

The speed shifts from twenty miles per hour to seventy as the twister charges toward the mutations. Entranced by the spinning cyclone, they make contact and instantly explode. Like fireworks on the ground, Eve lights up the entire valley in her destruction.

And then there are none.

She only feels the gentle thrum from the generators and the energy flowing through the power lines.

Eyes rolling into the back of her head, she slams into the ground.

Chapter 33

From within the Humvee, Eve can hear them talking. Somewhere in the back of her mind, the words are registering, but she is unable to move.

"Take her fucking cuffs off, you moron!" Maggie yells, followed by rustling. If Eve had to guess, West is holding her back.

"Just a precautionary measure," Martin placates. Yes, Martin is speaking now.

"She didn't attack any of us! She attacked *them*! Maybe if you stopped for two seconds and removed that huge stick out of your teeny tiny—"

"That doesn't change the fact that we don't know what we're dealing with."

"At least we know now why the solar cells didn't take!" Rowan chimes in sarcastically. He must be somewhere in the front. Leave it to Rowan to be cracking a joke right now.

Eve's head is in someone's lap, and they are soothingly running their fingers through her hair. Not male, *female*. Has to be

Beth. Eve highly doubts Sophia would be coming anywhere near her, especially now. At least her friend wasn't scared of her.

Friend. Beth is good friend.

Next thing she knows, she is being carried from the Humvee. Thrown over a shoulder, the blood pools in her skull from her inversion. It tingles, sending heat to her icy skin. Ever since... whatever that was, Eve has been freezing.

"Way to go, freak," a male voice whispers. Rowan.

She inversely spots the log structure, Evergreen, as he sets her carefully on a gurney. It starts to move. She can feel the different changes in light through her closed lids, hearing whispers from whoever they pass. She knows what they must be thinking.

What did Eve do this time?

She tries to smile but fails. Eve doesn't even know what Eve did.

Everyone is okay.

Is she okay? Probably not. But everyone else is. That is all that matters. Everyone that she loves is okay.

The gurney stops and she manages to crack open one eye. Rowan hovers above her. He looks funny from this angle.

"You're upside down," she mumbles.

"Maybe I am downside up?" he snorts.

"Aren't you scared of me?"

Rowan shakes his head, but Eve's pretty sure he is lying.

"I'm scared of me," she confesses, clumsily throwing her forearm over her face. The laboratory lights are obnoxiously bright.

"You're going to feel a pinch, but we need to replenish your fluid levels." Martin again. The laboratory. Eve thinks she has been spending way too much time in here lately.

"Rowan?"

"Yeah?"

"I don't think my dreams were dreams…." Eve mumbles.

A few minutes pass and Martin checks her vitals, injecting a few more things into her arms. She trusts Martin.

"I don't think they were either…" Rowan grates, his voice full of emotion.

The white room. Her gray skin. The tank, the shots, her parents. It's like a slideshow, and Eve is starting to see the big picture. Slide after slide, memory after memory, it's all coming together.

Eve has an inclination about what is wrong with her.

She hopes her theory isn't right.

Chapter 34

It's been five days. Five long, nerve-wracking days.

Eve is depressed. And bored. And angry that she is stuck in here, bored and depressed.

The Zappers have a prison of sorts. Accessible by yet another tunnel, leading to a cave, with four clear cells.

Eve is the guest of honor.

The other three are empty, but they are all identical. Cot. Sink with cold water only. A toilet. And that's all.

She has counted, literally counted, the flagstone pieces in the concrete floor. There are 137. Using the flimsy plastic toothbrush she's been left, she sticks it into her hair, tying up most of her greasy mane into a bun.

Eve is starting to smell.

Or just starting to smell worse than she did by day three.

A change of clothes would have been nice. She is still sporting the stained clothing she was wearing during her ride-along. You know, the one where she annihilated hundreds of Snappers at once with a tornado of doom…. Eve saved their lives, and now they're treating her like a murderer.

She is one.

But she murdered the bad guys. That should count for something.

Maybe she should be locked up, but it doesn't make her feelings hurt any less at their mistrust.

The only person she's seen is Beth. Quite literally, just seen. She brings Eve three meals a day, but keeps her head down, not uttering a word. Eve would rather be despised than treated like she's invisible, especially by someone she's close to. Beth won't even tell her how Maggie is doing, or if she's okay, so Eve stopped asking.

Left in this transparent cage, she has nothing to do but think.

One positive. The nightmares have stopped. Maybe they only have hit pause, but Eve's gotten more sleep in the past five days than she's had the entire year.

What must Luca think of her?

He wasn't the one to bring her to the lab after she fainted, she remembered that much. That was Rowan. Luca probably hates her again, which really isn't fair. He couldn't possibly hate her more than she hates herself right now.

Or as much as she hates Adel and Orion.

What kind of parents experiment on their own child? Maybe Eve and Maggie aren't even blood related. They could be some sort of test-tube babies…it would explain the physical differences between them.

Maybe Eve is a ticking time bomb? Rigged to explode at the exact right moment? Scary thought. Riley and the rest are probably right, keeping her locked up in here. If she was in their shoes, she would have done the same.

These are Eve's thoughts as the hours drag by.

Worrying about Maggie, wondering what everyone is thinking about her, and speculating about what has been done to her DNA.

And one more.

How *good* it felt.

When she got out of the car and pulled the energy from the air and the ground. She felt every molecule gathering. She felt every single Snapper, and she relished the moment when she overloaded their systems until they exploded. She enjoyed the massacre, and she would do it again, given the chance.

She wants to be set loose on those monsters, because she is a monster too.

It really takes one to know one.

Sitting cross-legged on the floor with her back to the hallway between the enclosures, the walls surrounding her start to rise, disconnecting from the floor. Almost falling backwards, she catches herself and rolls to stand, ready to defend herself if necessary.

But then there is Maggie. And Tate, and Martin.

Making eye contact, the cell isn't completely retracted before her sister ducks through and envelops her in a tight embrace.

"Oh my God, Eve, are you going to give me lice or something? What the heck!"

Stepping back, she inspects Eve's current state and Maggie is appalled.

"Just a precautionary measure," Martin justifies.

"Fuck your precautions. Look at her!"

Maggie stands in front of her protectively, daring Martin or Tate to approach. Noticing that Tate is holding something—it looks to be the high-tech cuffs, like the pair they placed on her in the car—Eve sighs.

She thought she was being let out, but Eve is apparently still a threat.

Stomping over to Tate, Maggie snatches the cuffs and marches right back to Eve.

"Hold out your arms. This is the only way they'll let you leave here. Don't worry, I have made all of their lives a living hell since they threw you in this shit bucket."

The satisfied smirk on Maggie's face lets Eve know that she isn't kidding. Eve can only imagine what Maggie has been up to in her absence.

Apparently a whole lot, as she notices a certain silver moonstone ring on her sister's right hand.

She has seen that ring before. As her sister struggles with her shackles, Eve can't help but ask, "Isn't that Lucia's?"

"Yup," Maggie replies, nonchalant.

"Did you steal it?"

"Nope."

"Find it and not return it? Because that's still stealing...."

"Wrong again."

"Well, did she give it to you?"

At this, Maggie snickers, pleased about something that has transpired.

"She isn't half bad, when you get to know her. And Lucia and Sophia have been kind of on your—our—side about Riley letting you out. Sophia 'wasn't ready to die' and is 'totally in your debt' after you went *Twister* on those mutations."

At this news, Eve's jaw drops, the cold metal of the cuffs finally tightening around her wrists.

"I wouldn't trust them just yet, they're more 'frenemies,' but Lucia is trying to buy my love, and I'm letting her."

Her task complete, Maggie turns to the guys and bellows, "Done, you idiots! Happy?"

She motions for Eve to start walking.

The cuffs are checked by Martin, who confirms they are indeed secured and activated. Only then does Eve follow the group away from the cells and through the way out. But instead of downwards, the way she was first led from Evergreen, Tate selects another tunnel heading up. Exiting, Eve squints from the morning sun as they step directly onto a flat outcrop at the base of a small mountain.

Eve can see Evergreen below.

Trying not to cry, she realizes that isn't where they are headed. The big clue being the helicopter that is right in front of them.

As hurt and confused as Eve is, she would give anything to be back there. Back in her room with Maggie. Back in Luca's arms.

"You have to be kidding me," Eve blurts.

Taking two black handkerchiefs from her pockets, Maggie flips Tate and Martin the bird before taking one and tying it around Eve's eyes. Blinded, she assumes that Maggie does the same to herself before the Quinns push them toward the helicopter. Instructing them when to step up, and when to duck their heads.

"Maybe, you should have gotten us into this contraption, and then had us put on these. Wouldn't that have made more sense?" Maggie snaps, but noise-canceling headphones are slid over their ears, and for the rest of the flight, both of the Abbott sisters only feel and hear a faint rumbling. The pressure changes as they drop elevations and smoothly land.

Being guided by what must be Tate's brutally large hands, Eve exits the helicopter. Their headphones are removed and their blindfolds, but the cuffs on Eve remain in place.

At first, she thinks they are in the middle of the forest near Evergreen, where she and Rowan had gone running. She thinks she recognizes this small clearing. Her gaze starts at the base of the trees, and then rises toward their branches.

And what she notices, in the trees, instantly changes her mind.

They aren't anywhere near Evergreen.

This place is something else entirely.

Chapter 35

"A treehouse? Really? Isn't this a bit excessive, even for you guys?" Maggie shields her face, studying the structures, partially hidden by the foliage.

"And Evergreen?" Eve asks, disappointed. While intrigued by the structures that seem to be floating between the massive trunks, part of her wants to go home.

Evergreen felt like home, even more so than Seattle ever did. A home in which she is no longer welcome.

"Whatever. So, how do we get from down here to up there? Stairs? Tate uses his big hairy arms to toss us as high as he can, and it's up to us to grab onto something?"

Noticing some signal that Eve and Maggie must have missed, both Tate and Martin nod their heads and move forward, beelining for a gargantuan oak. Arriving at where the trunk meets the soil, sure enough, a rectangular section of the tree opens, revealing a modern-looking elevator.

"Tree elevator? There's actually a tree elevator? Nice...." Maggie snorts, stepping inside first.

It's a tight fit with all four of them, and Eve can tell her fragrant aroma is causing issues. She tries not to fidget as everyone but her takes turns holding their breath.

Ding. The group reaches the only floor the elevator goes to, and the door opens. Stepping out, they are in the center of a large, pentagon-shaped room. The tree's trunk extends to the top and up through the roof, reaching even higher into the sky beyond.

Within this room there is a full spotless kitchen to the left. Couches, loveseats, and an actual large flatscreen TV on the right. Completing it, three round tables with chairs in the back for dining.

Eve forgets everything for a moment, taking in the wizardry of this place. An adult tree fort but with modern amenities. Noticing the second, wrap-around level with a rope railing, she wonders how you access it until she spots the wood ladder, attached to the tree trunk on the opposite side of the elevator, that connects to a short bridge.

"Can we remove the cuffs now? Big bad Eve here needs to be drowned in soap," Maggie requests.

Plopping on the tan leather couch, Maggie grabs a remote from a stand, and flips it on. She squeals, realizing what channel is playing.

"HBO! Eve! They have HBO! I'm never leaving here...."

Martin approaches Eve, holding a black tablet.

"Your cuffs are disabled, you can remove them, but a chip has been implanted into your spine. If you go beyond fifty feet of this spot, you will be terminated. If you show any irregularities that I or my team deem a threat, you will be terminated. Clear?"

Grabbing for her neck, Eve feels a small, tender spot right at the top of her first vertebrae. Great. Like she needed one more scar.

Exhaling, she shrugs, removing the cuffs and handing them to Martin. He takes them, heads back to the elevator, gets on, and it shuts, leaving them alone with Tate.

"Are you our babysitter?" Maggie inquires, laser focused on the cable channels as she rapidly flips between them.

"Yup."

"Sorry about that," she mumbles.

And then Tate moves to sit in one of the loveseats next to Maggie. His joints crack as he bends and plops down. Pulling a lever on the side, the footrest rises, and he sighs in contentment.

"I volunteered, actually," Tate offers, causing Maggie to hit the mute button.

"Not upset that you did. Better you than Martin. But can I ask what you guys plan on doing with us in this tree castle?"

"Martin will be back soon. Talk to him." Tate brushes Maggie off, watching the silent baseball game as a pitcher throws his third strike.

Eve doesn't want to interrupt. In her time in solitude, it feels odd to speak at all. But she really does need to find the washroom, if only to stop the itching.

"Is there someplace I can bathe?" Eve asks softly.

"Yeah, see the door next to the kitchen? Walk out, and across. Next building over...."

The baseball game is un-muted, and Maggie and Tate are entranced. It seems that Tate has been devoid of television for even longer than they have.

Turning the handle, the wind assails her, rocking the bridge from side to side. Her stomach turns as she takes her first step onto the swaying structure, reminding herself to not look down. A woven netting has been installed around the bridge, so there really is no way of accidentally falling, but still. Powering her way over to the smaller pentagon-shaped building it leads to, she steps through the entrance. Finding a sliding panel hidden in the doorframe, Eve rolls it closed, locking herself inside.

The room is basic. A giant tub in the wooden floor and a cabinet stacked with towels. Water running from a hole in the ceiling on the left into a drain on floorboards must serve as the "sink."

What truly takes her breath away is the view. The paned windows gift her with a perfect perspective of the treetops and the sun, barely visible along the ridgeline beyond. The sky is pink and orange, covered in soft fluffy clouds with nowhere to be in a hurry.

When she dies, Eve wants to be buried in this bathtub.

Especially when she finds out that, yes, there is hot water. Within a sliding compartment, opening in the floor next to the tub, she finds every toiletry that she requires—including stacks upon stacks of various-sized clothing. The Zappers really do think of everything.

Clean and refreshed, Eve walks with slightly more confidence across the suspended bridge once more.

Stepping through and shutting out the wind, she is surprised to see that they have visitors.

Riley and Beth are standing in the kitchen. Martin is back as well. They are huddled, their voices muffled as they discuss—more than likely—her.

And there is Luca.

His back is to Eve, his hands in his pockets as he stands near Maggie and Tate. The eldest Quinn must have heard her come in, but he doesn't acknowledge her entrance.

"Luca?" she calls out, desperate for him to turn around.

His muscles tense, but he stays facing the television. It is as she had feared.

She and Luca are no more.

"Eve, good to see you. Will you join us?" Riley motions for her to approach, taking a seat at one of the dining tables. Beth looks kindly at Eve, patting the spot next to her.

Soon, everyone is in one of the chairs, and the TV has been flipped off. Eve feels like she has been punched in the gut. Staring at the table, she waits for Riley to lead their makeshift meeting.

"First off, Eve, I apologize for these conditions. It's not that we don't trust you, but you can understand our need for caution..." Riley begins.

"I also apologize for your quarters the past week. Martin needed to run some tests and get to the bottom of what occurred at the power plant. He thinks he's discovered the cause, but we are in entirely new territory with you."

"I'm a hybrid, aren't I?" Eve whispers, already knowing the answer.

Silence. A needle could drop and they would all hear it.

Martin sees this as his cue to chime in.

"In layman's terms, yes. Adel and Orion have somehow halted a full transformation. Hitting pause on your mutation, you are not one or the other. You're somewhere in the middle. We are also aware that you didn't know. You were telling the truth when we questioned you right after the attack, based on software analysis of your vitals during your divulsions. I am still puzzling out how exactly your parents were able to mask your memories. They might have inserted a sort of block in your hippocampus...."

"Martin," Riley interjects.

"Apologies."

Riley takes the lead once more.

"We do not believe you are a threat. If anything, you might be the tipping point in our war. But we are unsure of your capabilities, and we are concerned about areas in your makeup that might have been...tampered with."

"You think my parents might have installed some sort of 'failsafe,'" Eve mutters, again, spot on.

At least Riley is honest when he answers, "Yes. We are concerned that this was their plan all along. Abandon you, we take you in, you win over our trust, and when the time is right, you turn on us."

"You're dumb as rock if you think that Eve is anything but good. You saw what she did at the power plant!" Maggie says, coming to her defense.

"No, Maggie, he's right..." Eve agrees, placating her sibling.

Maggie flashes her a look that says, "No, he isn't," but backs down.

"What now?" Eve asks, resigned.

"Now, we see what you can do." It's Luca who speaks this time, but every word is acid.

Eve now wishes she was back in her glass-like cell, in the mountain, alone.

Instead of here, with witnesses to her heartbreak.

She has tried to prepare herself for this moment, convince herself that Luca's reaction was to be expected. But if she hadn't gotten out of that car, and did what she did, there would be no more Luca.

Either way, she would have lost him.

But it doesn't make the pain of the loss any easier.

Chapter 36

Sharing a room on the second floor with Beth and Maggie, Eve tosses and turns in her top bunk. The room can sleep six, three bunks on either side, and Eve chose the uppermost mattress on the opposite side of the space, Beth and her little sister claiming the bottom and middle adjacent.

Unsure of the hour, tear after tear rolls from Eve's swollen eyes, onto her hair and the pillow below her head. Silent in her misery, she is surprised when Maggie sits up, throws off her covers, and climbs down a ladder to the pine board flooring.

Pattering feet, she then climbs all the way up to Eve, peeking her head over the low railing.

"Scoot."

Eve obliges, a sob unwillingly escaping.

More pattering of feet, climbing, and Beth joins them as well, crawling over to the other side of Eve, smacking her head on the low ceiling in the process.

"Ouch, man!" Beth giggles, holding her temple as she and Maggie sandwich Eve in the middle.

All three lay on their backs, side by side, waiting for Eve to talk when she is ready.

"I am so sorry...." Eve's voice cracks, the depth of her sorrow on full display.

"For what? Saving mine and my brothers' lives out there?" Beth says with total conviction.

"Really? I thought... You didn't say anything to me in my cell," Eve says cautiously.

Beth punches one of Eve's pillows, fluffing it. Turning on her side to face her, she says, "I was instructed not to speak to you. And I was on camera. After you...did whatever you did, Evergreen was in chaos, so I had to fall in line. Eve, Riley and anyone that isn't trusting you right now is a fool."

"Especially the tall stupid one with the shaved head," Maggie growls, all three of them knowing she is referring to Luca.

"Wait, before you cast judgment, there is something that you need to hear," Beth starts, cautiously. "And I honestly never planned on telling either of you, but I think you need to know this, to truly understand him."

Eve quiets, waiting for whatever this latest secret might reveal.

"You may have noticed—we never talk about our parents. Maybe you assumed that they were on assignment somewhere, or we're not very close, but that's not the case...."

Eve can tell that this is a difficult topic, but Beth proceeds.

"Your parents and our parents were...close. They came up at Evergreen together, were assigned to the same pod in Seattle, and started having children around the same time. When Adel and Orion were discovered doing what they were doing—playing Frankenstein only to create stronger mutants—they assumed that the raid on their lab was our parents' doing. That they were the ones who ratted them out. The same night your parents disappeared, our parents were found in Saintsville, in the house across from your grandmother's. Both of their throats had been slit."

Eve and Maggie gasp. In the darkness, their hands cover their mouths as both sisters try to sit up in the cramped space.

Now everyone, not just Eve, is crying.

"Our parents killed yours? I am so, so sorry…." Maggie reaches across Eve and squeezes Beth's arm.

Begging for Beth to believe her, Eve adds, "We didn't know, I swear, we didn't…."

But Beth's shushing silences both of the Abbotts.

"You and Maggie are innocent. You are good, and loving, and fiercely devoted to those you care about. You're nothing like Adel or Orion, and I trust both of you with my life."

"Careful… Maybe just trust me? Eve is unreliable at the moment…."

Thanks to Maggie's comment, all the girls erupt in giggles.

But then Eve stops. Freezes. She slaps her hands to the girls' mouths, silencing them.

Snappers.

She can feel them, on the bridge and the walkways.

One is right outside their quarters.

The hinges on their door starts to squeak, and slowly, ever so slowly, it opens.

Beth stealthily moves to lay across the mattress until she is peeking through the railings toward the entrance. Maggie and Eve follow suit.

Steam and smoke start to fill the room as a giant, scorpion-like creature slithers through, stopping in the center.

With two stingers instead of one, the all-black insect is the size of a lion as it unfolds. In the middle of its pincers is a human-like face. A face exactly like the smoker Eve had first encountered. Its long neck makes three loud clicks, tilting to look at the girls.

The hairs raise on Eve's arms. It's staring directly at them.

Without warning, Beth screams "*Snappers!*" and leaps from the top, landing and rolling so that she is directly in front of the monstrosity...putting herself immediately in harm's way.

Chapter 37

M aggie and Eve do not hesitate. Quickly climbing down three or four rungs each, they jump the rest of the way, landing close to Beth.

So far, their parents' latest concoction seems to be waiting for something. Its eight legs shuffle, moving slightly backwards, then slightly forwards. It hisses at them, sending Eve's body into overdrive. From within the treehouse, they hear chaos being unleashed. Lights flash and dim, yelling, the boys' electrically charged superweapons indicating that their backup is delayed.

The boys, whatever they're fighting, currently have their hands full.

"What I need…is in my bunk…." Beth snarls.

"How can we help? Distraction?" Maggie's eyes dart around the space, looking for anything that could be used to buy Beth some time.

Then they hear it. What sounds like thousands of nails tapping on glass. The sound grows louder and louder, until more of the scorpion-like creatures pour into the room. Crawling up the walls and pushing the girls to the far back, cutting them off from the only exit. A single window is placed high on the wall and unreachable, but at least the moon is bright, granting them a clear picture of what they're about to face.

"We are seriously screwed," Maggie groans.

Then one, two, the entire room starts to hiss. The noise is deafening. Eve knows, somewhere deep inside of her, that they are gearing up for the kill.

Then she feels it. A few sparks erupt on her exposed areas, extinguishing as quickly as they manifest. Her skin starts to heat, and total calm takes over, only to be interrupted by a stabbing pain in her neck, dropping her directly to her knees.

"Dammit! Damn Martin and his stupid chip!" Eve roars, clawing at her neck.

"What are you doing? Eve, stop!" Beth begs.

She does stop; she freezes.

Every single cell in her body is at her command, as she sends positively charged molecules to surround the chip. She feels it, small and flat, connected to her spinal column. It doesn't have a chance. Attacking it from every angle, surrounding it, she fries the chip, disabling it with ease.

Then she smiles.

The darkness comes once more.

Small tendrils of smoke start to crawl from her fingers. They are beautiful as they extend, twisting and flowing carefully outwards. Paper thin, they split, and split again, until each branch of her intricate web dangles directly in front of each one of her brethren.

She feels their confusion. Hypnotized by the smoking, glowing lines, her trap begins to resemble a honeycomb, the lines connecting, spreading, and connecting again, until each mutation is wrapped in their own electric cage.

The hissing turns to shrieks as a few touch the glowing lines, only to lose a pincer or a leg. Piles of mutant dust collect around them, raining from the monstrosities positioned on the ceiling. And then her cages start to shrink. And shrink, and shrink, and shrink. Eve relishes in their agonizingly slow demise as she feels their fear and feeds on it.

The shrieks intensify to a deafening howl as Beth and Maggie cover their ears, until the room explodes into a cloud of ash.

Eve's eyes fade from black to clear blue. Her raised hair, moving in non-existent wind starts to lower. Shaky, but she doesn't black out after this episode. Good, Eve is making progress.

Helping her sister to her feet, she adamantly says, "No one is putting a chip in my neck again."

"I'd like to see them try…." Maggie coughs, lifting her night shirt to cover the lower half of her face, acting as a sort of filter in the foggy room.

Beth, coughing as well, mimics Maggie, swatting at the thick dust coating every inch of the dormitory. She manages to say, "Who are you?!" between wheezes.

"I have no clue." Eve's answer is so honest that they all erupt in laughter.

Chapter 38

Eve didn't just take care of the scorpions in their space. She had exterminated every threat, inside and out, all at once.

Nausea starts to roll over her in waves, causing her to put her palms on her knees. Maggie hurries over, thinking her injured.

"I'm fine. I might just throw up," Eve whispers hoarsely.

"She needs water, she is probably dehydrated again. I'll be right back!"

Beth sprints in her mutant-covered pajamas out the door, passing Luca and Tate on the way.

"Everyone is fine! Eve just needs fluids!" she yells from somewhere on the outside railing.

What Beth fails to notice are the weapons that Tate and Luca are still holding. Martin and Riley soon join them, as they stalk into the room, forming a *V*, with Riley at the helm. Eve soon learns Riley's weapon of choice—a boomerang. Dwarfed in size by his muscle-bound arms.

Seeing these warriors in their full glory, tattoos red and alive, they are one with their artillery. Eve can't help but feel a pang of sadness. She'll never be like them. They need their guns and knives—where she, Eve, only needs herself.

She is the weapon.

Maggie and Eve hear Beth cry out, "Wait, no! What are you doing?" hurrying through the doorway, holding two partially full glasses. Most of the water having spilled in her haste.

"You were warned what would happen if you did not comply, Miss Abbott. You knew the consequences, yet you disobeyed a direct order. We can do this here, or outside, away from your sister. I will give you the choice."

Maggie gasps, and she isn't the only one.

Beth drops the cups she is holding as they shatter.

Luca lowers his gun in shock and Tate his blades. Even rule-abiding Martin glances between his siblings, unsure of how to proceed. Their leader is going off script—the Quinns had not been informed that Riley intended to end Eve's life because of her disobedience.

"Riley…no. We are not killing her." The menace in Luca's voice is a clear threat.

"This is insane bro, I'm not doing this…." Tate chimes in as well, stepping out of the *V*, his blades slowing to a stop.

"You. Will. Obey. A. *Direct. Order*!" Spit flies from Riley's mouth like a rabid dog.

The nausea worsening, Eve has had quite enough of this. She steps forward, raises her hands, and before any of them have time to react, Eve flicks her wrist and their weapons flash white. Each solider dropping them to the floor, in reaction to Eve giving them a jolt.

Riley roars and goes to charge, but Eve stops him in his tracks just by holding out her sparking hand. They dance on her fingertips, daring him to come closer.

Riley is dumbfounded. Rigid, he is frozen in shock.

Maggie claps and whistles, leaning against the back wall next to Beth.

"Don't mess with my sister, Ri-Ri!" she taunts.

"But the chip…how?" Riley stumbles, at a loss for words.

"I put it in a microwave and hit start. I am grateful to you, all of you, and my time spent at Evergreen, but I think my sister and I will be going now."

"What about West?" Maggie whines.

"He can choose. With them, or with us. But I am sick of being a puppet. I cut the strings, time to leave."

Another voice chimes in behind her.

"I'm coming with you." Beth steps forward, defiant.

"*Absolutely*—" Riley begins to bellow, but stops again, barely containing his fury.

And then Eve feels it. Every hair on her body rises as she turns her back on Riley and the rest, facing toward her beautiful little sister.

"Maggie, come over here," she instructs, staring at something that only she can see.

"No way. I'm good, thank you!" Maggie is enjoying watching the soap opera unfold.

"Maggie. Get away from the wall!"

Eve's hair starts to rise, and all color drains from her irises, replaced with an inky darkness.

That can only mean one thing.

One step. Maggie only takes one step before the wood paneling splinters and blasts open.

Time stops. Everything seems to be in happening in slow motion as Eve watches massive scaly talons breaking through. One grabs Maggie before shooting straight into the air.

But not before Eve saw someone riding on the flier. Someone who has haunted her every second of every day, since she had left Eve behind.

Adel is there, in all black, the lines of her tattoos a puzzling purple instead of the red Eve had grown accustomed to. She sees her mother, their eyes locking for a split second.

And her mother's smile is victorious.

Someone is screaming. Long and loud, the sound of total and utter devastation.

Eve realizes that it's her.

She can already feel the flier traveling farther, and farther away, too fast for her to catch up. And then nothing.

Dawning realization hits, as her head snaps toward Beth.

"What is today?" Eve demands.

"Huh?"

Beth is confused, unsure why in this moment it matters.

"Today, today! What is today's date?!"

It is Martin that finally answers.

"It's the fourteenth, I believe. Of November."

"Ah-ha," is all Eve utters, before heading with purpose to the built-in closet next to her bunk and throwing it open.

She grabs a duffel bag, and a change of warm dark clothing, stuffing whatever she can manage before zipping it closed. Not caring that she still has an audience, she throws off her soiled pajamas, hurriedly replacing them with daytime clothing.

In shock, all of the other occupants just watch her, many wondering if she has finally cracked.

Luca is the first to move in her direction.

"Why does the day matter, Eve?" His voice is soothing, like someone talking to a feral cat they want to tame.

"Because today is Maggie's birthday. She's seventeen."

Zipping her windbreaker and grabbing her duffel bag, she plans on walking straight past him—but his warm hand stops her, gently clasping her bicep.

"Where are you going?" Luca asks.

"To give Maggie a present. It is her birthday, after all."

"And what might that be?" he inquires again, still holding her tightly.

"Isn't it obvious? I am going to hunt Adel and Orion down. And then, I am going to kill them."

Yanking her bicep free, she pushes past Luca, and is almost to the doorway when she hears him yell, "Wait!"

"Dammit Eve, I'm coming with you." Luca jogs from the room, heading to gather his things. Beth is way ahead of him, already packed, and changing as well. She smiles at Eve and nods, letting her know her answer.

"I need at least fifteen, and then I should be ready to go as well." Martin furiously types on a tablet he has seemingly magicked from thin air.

Riley begins to shake in rage, his eyes maniacal as he yells, "No, you are not!"

But everyone ignores him, having already decided that Riley is no longer in charge.

Eve is.

Eve.

Beth.

Martin.

Tate.

Luca.

Five is better than one when preparing to murder two.

She had been right to trust the Quinns. They just needed to hurry. Maggie's clock is ticking.

"Martin, do you have a phone?" she asks.

"I do," he says. Reaching into his pocket, he hands it over willingly.

Dialing a few numbers, she holds the phone to her ear, and waits.

"Jill. It's me, Eve. I need your help."